RIDING OUT THE STORM
BELOW THE SALT
BOOK SIX

ELIZABETH ROSE

OLIVERHEBERBOOKS

CHAPTER I
HYTHE, ENGLAND, AUGUST, 1375

E dgar Blackmore, known as Gar by his family and friends, whistled softly, eyeing up *Lady Josefina's* voluptuous curves and swells. Totally captivated by such perfection and irresistible beauty, he was unable to look away.

"Now that's one hell of a lady," Gar said in admiration, speaking to his cousin, Rook Blake, who was standing on the docks next to him. With them was Gar's half-sister, Eleanor, as well as their cousin, Martine. "Feast your eyes upon her flawlessness. Drink in her extremely desirable elegance and creation. She's so... big!" He whistled lowly once again. "Have you ever seen another like her?"

Lady Josefina truly was engaging. She was also every-thing Gar had always coveted but had not been lucky enough to get his hands on, until now. He'd noticed her on the docks recently and had coveted her from the first time he laid eyes on her. Now his dream was about to come true and he couldn't hold back his excitement.

"Stop drooling," scoffed Rook with a shake of his head, causing his long black hair to swish back and forth. "It's downright embarrassing." Rook's eyes darted back and forth. It was no secret that he cared what type of impression they made on the commoners. Then again, they were noble. They did have a certain reputation to maintain, Gar supposed.

Gar had been hired by the wealthy international trade merchant, Donald Waterman, to do a job that would place the *Lady Josefina* right into his hands for at least the next few weeks, hopefully longer. It was just where he wanted to be. God's eyes, he couldn't wait. This was the chance of a lifetime. He'd actually have the opportunity to climb atop this beauty and go for a wild ride.

"Gar! Will you please stop gawking at that stupid boat and listen to me when I'm speaking to you?" scolded Eleanor, placing her hands on her hips in frustration. Eleanor was married to a man who was first a noble, then a hangman, and now a noble once again. Stray bits of her bright red hair escaped her headpiece, the thin strands being blown about in the strong wind. There was always some sort of breeze or wind present at the docks, coming off the channel. It was also a bustling place with some very questionable types of people.

Gar's head snapped around and his eyes narrowed. "It's a ship, Eleanor. A ship," he corrected her in a stern voice. "The *Lady Josefina* is so much more than just a boat, so please don't ever refer to her as such again." Gar's attention drifted back to the huge craft rising majestically from the water, paling the image of any of the other vessels in the harbor. That is, all except for his father's ship, the *Champion*, which was about the same size. Gar's father was Lord Warden of the Cinque Ports, so that was to be expected.

"Ship, boat, what does it matter?" asked Eleanor throwing her hands in the air aimlessly. "It's all the same to me." She ended her opinion with a sigh.

"To say such a thing is blasphemy, dear sister." Gar turned back toward Eleanor once more and scowled to show her his disappointment. "You have no idea what you're saying. This is the ship of my dreams!" His arm flayed out in front of him as he pointed at the *Lady Josefina*. "I've just been hired as the ship's captain for a mission. Don't you understand how important an opportunity like this really is?"

The ship was being loaded by the dock workers. Last-minute barrels and boxes filled with food and other goods would be sold at the trade fair. Scarborough was their first stop, and one of the busiest places for a trade fair. This was an international trade ship so Gar was sure the cargo also included spices, silks, and perhaps even more expensive things like gold and silver jewelry. This cargo was special. Mainly nobles would be interested in most of it and the only ones able to afford the things. Selling to nobles was probably why Donald Waterman was rich enough to afford such an elaborate trade ship.

However, it didn't matter much to Gar what the ship carried or if it was even transporting anything at all. It's hold could be full or even empty. It didn't matter to him in the least. All he could think about was the fact he'd soon be captaining the best and probably fastest ship on the sea.

"He's so ridiculous, and acting like a besotted fool," Martine whispered to Eleanor. Gar overheard her complaint.

"Nay!" He slowly lowered his arm. "What is ridiculous is

that you two ladies are nobles and should be nowhere near the docks. Yet, here you are standing boldly amongst the wharf rats and whores as if you were naught but peasants. Go back to Saltwood Castle! The docks are not meant for fragile noblewomen. Go home to stitch tapestries in the ladies solar where you belong."

That didn't sit well with either of the women. Their anger at what he said showed on their faces. Gar already regretted not choosing his words more carefully.

"Fragile noblewomen?" both Martine and Eleanor said in unison. By the tone of their voices and the looks on their screwed-up faces, Gar realized he probably should have held his tongue. The women in his family seemed to have trouble acting like noblewomen of their status should. Instead of being obedient and silent, they all had their own opinions on things and never had any trouble letting everyone know. He supposed he should be used to it since his mother, at one time, was the worst. Having been stolen as a baby and raised by pirates, she had to learn how to act and speak like a noblewoman once she married Gar's Uncle Garrett, who was now Gar's father.

"What I meant is that Father and Mother won't be happy that you two left the security of the castle and came here to such a dangerous place. I only have your safety in mind."

"Aye, I'm sure that's what it is," said Eleanor sarcastically, looking less than amused.

"Why are you two even here at all?" Gar asked them once again. "I hardly think it is to wish me luck and see me off on my journey."

"There is good reason for us being here," Martine

answered with a sniff. "But you wouldn't know since you don't ever listen to a word we say." She nodded, including Eleanor as part of the *we*.

"Now, now. That is naught but a lie," he mumbled. "I hear every word. Even though I would rather not." He said the last part softly to himself, but speaking aloud.

"Hearing and listening are two different things," Martine pointed out. "With the way you act around the ladies, it is no wonder you're twenty-four years of age and still not married."

That took Gar by surprise. He wasn't expecting her to be so brash as to say that to his face, even if he knew his family members talked about it behind his back all the time. It was true, he was the eldest of the cousins and still single. However, he could be married if he really wanted to be. He'd just never found a lady who interested him enough to make him want to take his vows. Gar cleared his throat and answered.

"Well, since most of what you two talk about is naught but idle chatter and unimportant, I admit, I sometimes make a conscious decision at times not to fully listen. But then, I'm not really missing anything important, am I?"

"Mayhap you should at least try to listen once in a while and get your head out of the clouds," warned Eleanor.

"Mayhap you two should listen to what I have to say as well. For instance, look at the way the *Lady Josefina* sways back and forth in the breeze." He put his attention on what was important once again. "It's just like the rocking of a baby. The sea is her mother." He pointed at the ship once again, but the girls rolled their eyes and looked the other way. "The motion is almost like a dance," he continued. "It's nature's sweet dance on the exciting waters that lead a man to thrilling adventures and new destinations. You realize, it's no different than moving over the floor of a great hall with a beautiful lady on my arm. Only this time, the lady is so much better. This time she won't expect me to listen to her idle chatter." He ended with a satisfying smile and nod, knowing this would rile the women. Gar was sometimes a trouble-maker and did things on purpose to make his girl cousins and sister flustered. Well, after this, the girls were sure to want to leave.

Eleanor clucked her tongue, sounding like a hen. Martine sighed like a bored child. Gar, for the life of him, couldn't figure out why Rook had brought them along today or why he was staying silent. Gar's cousins were visiting his family at Saltwood Castle, but the women should be at the keep right now. And certainly not at the docks. All they were proving to be was a big distraction.

"Gar, the ladies aren't wrong," Rook finally spoke, shocking Gar and breaking him away from his thoughts.

"What did you say?" asked Gar, giving Rook his full attention.

Rook shrugged. "I do have to admit that you admire ships the way most men eye up pretty women. It's not normal. Neither is it admirable for a nobleman to act in this manner."

"Mayhap not, but it's what interests me," Gar told him. "Besides, it's my job. I'm a sea captain. Ships are supposed to take my undivided attention. Don't you understand?"

"You do captain the king's ships on occasion, that is true," Rook responded. "But bid the devil, Cousin, you are insufferable! The way you are drooling over this ship is going to make people think you're naught more than a bloody pirate." Once again, Rook's eyes scanned the busy dock.

"A pirate?" That statement was a stab to Gar's heart. He worked hard to hold back his anger at hearing this. He had been born on a pirate ship and raised by pirates and whores when he was very young. It was a sore spot with him. That had been a dark time in his life. But things were different now. Now, he'd been accepted as the true nobleman he was, and he didn't want anyone ever calling him a pirate again! Plus, pirates killed his birth father before Gar had ever known him. Nay, he hated pirates and didn't ever want to be associated with them again.

"I'm sorry. I had no right to say that. I didn't mean anything by it." Rook raised his hands in surrender. "Everyone knows you're not a pirate and neither is your mother. I mean... not really. Not anymore."

Disappointment filled Gar. "I didn't expect this from you, Rook." Gar wasn't talking about the pirate insult. Yes, that upset him, but there was something else that made him even more on edge right now. He was more upset that Rook didn't see the importance of this ship to him. Gar had hoped that at least his male cousin would understand him. After all, women couldn't care less about ships or fighting or weapons, but men thought differently than silly wenches. Men knew the important things in life. Or mayhap this was only what he deemed to be true and it really meant nothing to anyone else but him. Suddenly, he was no longer sure.

"I said, I'm sorry. I'm only trying to help you," Rook tried to convince him.

"Help me? How?" He glanced at Rook from the sides of his eyes.

"Gar, I overheard my father talking with yours last night. As soon as you return from this one last trip on the water, you're to be betrothed and married. You will be expected to settle down and have heirs."

Gar laughed at first, thinking that his cousin was jesting. That is, until he realized he was serious. "I see." He cleared his throat and scuffed the ground with the toe of his boot. "You're not jesting about this, are you?"

Rook slowly shook his head. "You knew it was coming sooner or later. But I assure you, being married isn't all that bad."

"Rook, I have a job on the water. I'll never settle down into a manor house like you. I like to travel about. I can't stay in one place, it'll drive me mad."

"About your job," said Rook, looking extremely uncomfortable. He looked at the ground as he spoke. "I hear that is all about to change as well."

"What do you mean? I captain the ships that King Edward sends out on his secret missions. I've been doing that for years now."

"Well... not anymore," said Rook. "It seems the king's counsel has advised him not to let you continue to work for him. The whole issue of you being raised with— I mean— some of them still think you're a—" Rook made a face and shrugged. "It's just that wagging tongues have taken the king's ear, that's all."

"Pirate is what you're trying to say without really saying it, isn't it?" asked Gar. "Do some of the nobles and those of the king's court really consider me a pirate?"

"Nay, of course not. I never said that." Rook waved a careless hand through the air. "I'm sure there are other reasons."

"It's all gossip and not true. It's no different than the wagging tongues of women," said Gar, jerking his head toward the girls.

"I resent that, Brother," sneered Eleanor. "And don't forget your mother is my mother as well. Yet, no one calls me a pirate! You've brought this on yourself with the way you act."

"You weren't born on a pirate ship, like I was," Gar snapped. "Besides, your father is the Lord Warden of the Cinque Ports. No one would dare make an ill reference to you."

"He's your father too, now," Eleanor reminded him.

"He is," said Gar, feeling an emptiness in his heart for the father he never knew. Lord Garrett was his late father's brother and took over as his father, and Gar appreciated that. But it wasn't the same. Gar often wondered about his true father and longed to know him, but never had.

"Talk to Uncle Garrett about what the king said," Rook told Gar. "He'll tell you what I've heard is true."

It hurt that the king hadn't given this information directly to Gar. Instead, he had to hear it from others. "Mayhap it is true, but I don't know why my father hasn't said something to me about it by now." Gar felt anxious and angry at the same time. Were people afraid to talk to him for some reason?

"Father knew it would upset you," Eleanor told him. "That is why he wanted to soften the blow by setting you up to sail this boat first." She nodded to the *Lady Josefina*.

"Ship, Eleanor. Ship," he said through clenched teeth. "And what do you mean *he* was responsible for this job? I received a letter from the owner, asking me to captain it for him."

The *Lady Josefina* was a large, carrack ship, usually seen in Portugal but not yet in England. It was bigger than the normal clinker-built cog. The vessel could hold at least two-hundred tuns in the hold, mayhap more. And while most ships only had one main sail, *The Lady Josefina* had not one, but three! With that kind of sail power, that must be. Surely, it had to be a sturdy and steadfast ship on the sea. This vessel was much too elite for a common trade ship. How had the owner become so lucky? King Edward III would be sure to want this ship as a warship as soon as he heard about it. Gar's excitement to tell the king quickly faded, remembering that he would no longer be in King Edward's service. And why should he want to tell the king anything when the man obviously kept his secrets from him?

Nay, he decided. The *Lady Josefina* was much too wonderful to be used as a vessel of war and he wouldn't let that happen. He would never tell the king about it as long as he lived.

The ship had carved scrolls and designs that started at the bow and led all the way down the tall sidewalls to the aft. The wood looked smooth, with a sheen in the sunlight. The masts were strong and the sails brilliant. There was a forecastle, or raised deck at the front of the ship and a sterncastle at the back with the captain's cabin below. The construction was impeccable and showed true talent. It was not only a sailing vessel but also a work of art.

The ship displayed a figurehead carved from wood

attached to the underside of the bow. It was the top half of a beautiful woman with long, flowing hair over rounded, full bare breasts. A woman like this in real life could drop any man to his knees at just one glance. Even from this far away, the ship was the most impressive thing he'd ever laid his eyes on. The shipwright, the man who'd designed and built this trade ship, had to be the most brilliant man alive.

Gar's passion had always been sailing ships ever since he was old enough to help hoist the sails. He supposed it was in his blood. He truly did love life on the water. He even chose sailing over being trained as a knight, because of the way it made him feel. Gar felt free and alive out there on the water. With the wind in his hair and the sun on his face, he felt as if he could conquer the world. It was a feeling he never had being on land. On occasion, Gar even helped the Barons of the Cinque Ports patrol the channel, keeping it free from pirates. Shouldn't that have proved he was a worthy man?

The thought that King Edward wouldn't require his services anymore already haunted him. And hearing also that upon returning from this trip, he'd be betrothed and married to a lady he had never even met, made him feel trapped already. Still, he was determined not to let anything bring down his spirits when he was about to take the sail of his life.

"Where will you be heading?" asked Rook curiously, pulling him from his thoughts.

"First stop is the trade fair at Scarborough," Gar reported. "From there, we'll head to a marketplace in Dunbar, Scotland, where bartering will take place. After that, we will be heading across the sea to Denmark for more trade. It will be a lengthy trip."

"Cousin Lark is visiting in Dunbar with her husband, Lord Dustin and their daughter, Florie," Martine told him, sounding excited for some reason.

"That's nice," said Gar, wondering why she would even tell him or why she thought he should care. He would be working. Gar wouldn't have time for casual visits. This was a job and he needed to stay focused on the reasons he'd been hired.

"Did you know that Lark is pregnant?" Eleanor asked him.

"I know now," mumbled Gar, not paying much attention to the women's chatter. Children weren't at the top of his list of interests right now.

"Lark has invited me to meet her there and visit with her in Scotland," Martine continued talking.

"Uh huh," said Gar, his attention back on the ship and the crew loading the supplies. These weren't men he knew or was used to traveling with. He'd met the crew only briefly, but wanted to talk to them more before setting sail. Time was running out. He turned to speak to Rook. "This all came about so quickly, that I haven't even had time to meet the merchant who hired me. Plus, I've only spoken briefly to my crew."

"Take the day to get to know them," suggested Rook. "It would be a good idea."

"I can't," said Gar. "I was instructed by the owner that it is of utmost importance that the ship sets sail today. In order to make it to the trade fair in time, I suppose. I'm just waiting for Donald Waterman to show up, and we're leaving as soon as he arrives."

"What's your cargo?" asked Rook.

Gar wasn't totally sure. "It's all on the orders my father left for me before he went away this morning. I was still sleeping. I haven't had a moment to study it yet." Gar patted his tunic with the parchment tucked inside.

"Did you say Uncle Garrett left?" asked Rook.

"Yes. It seems there are pirates on the North Sea causing trouble again. He had to call in all the Barons of the Cinque Ports to discuss the matter and take action. He said we'll talk when we both return." He'd been so excited to see the ship, that he'd only skimmed his orders. But it was a simple trip to trade fairs, so what did it even matter? His only concern was captaining the ship and to get them safely to their destinations.

"Let me see that parchment." Rook held out his hand. Gar grumbled but retrieved the parchment and handed it to his cousin.

The heat of the late summer sun warmed Gar's face while the breeze blowing through his long black hair cooled him at the same time. Bid the devil, maritime life made him feel so alive. He couldn't wait to set sail and let the smell of salty air fill his senses. His eyes closed and a smile turned up the corners of his mouth. Life was good right now, no matter what might happen tomorrow. Gar usually lived for the day, so this would be no different. He raised his arms above his head, feeling happier than he had in a long while.

"What the hell is the matter with him?" he heard his cousin Robin's voice and opened his eyes to see not only

Robin, but also Robin's new wife, Sage, standing there looking at him as if they thought he were addled.

Sage was a small woman with strawberry-blonde hair and bright green eyes. She knew all about healing with herbs. She'd saved Robin's life when he fell through the ice on the lake after rescuing her from bandits. They fell in love after that. Even though Robin was a noble and Sage only a commoner, they ended up getting married. It seems they'd fallen into the same trap as his other cousins, Raven, Rook, Lark, and even his sister, Eleanor, who were all nobles, but married beneath their status, or from below the salt. This upset Gar's uncle, Lord Corbett Blake, to no end. Corbett insisted they all needed to marry nobles to keep the family name from being sullied once again. Actually, Corbett's parents were the ones who'd sullied the family name to begin with, and it seemed the harder Corbett tried to change things, the worse they became.

"What's wrong with our cousin is that he's just met the next ship he'll sail and he's already fallen in love with her," said Rook with a chuckle, scanning the parchment in his hands.

"Forget the ship for a minute and come back to land," teased Robin snapping his fingers in Gar's face. "You're creating quite a scene with the excitement you have about that vessel!"

Gar's smile slowly faded and his gaze darted back and forth. Unfortunately, he realized that what Robin said was true. There were many dockworkers and fishermen staring at him. Some of the whores who made the docks their work-place whispered to each other behind their hands. He had no doubt the gossip was about him this time. Now he regretted showing such excitement when he should have kept it hidden. These landlubbers wouldn't understand anything about sailing and the sea, so why bother thinking anyone could know how he felt? He slowly lowered his arms to his sides.

"I've accepted a job to sail the *Lady Josefina*," Gar explained, nodding at the vessel.

"Yes, I've heard." Robin nodded as well.

Gar was surprised that Robin knew about his next mission since it only came to be this morning. But with family members visiting his parents right now at Saltwood Castle, word seemed to travel quickly. "Do you also know it's a trade ship and that I'm stopping at several trade fairs up the coast?"

"I do," said Robin. "Sage told me all about it."

"Sage told you?" Gar thought it was interesting how women always knew about things first. He supposed it was because they liked to gossip.

"I am friends with the merchant who owns this ship," Sage explained.

Gar's head jerked around. "You are?" This confused as well as impressed him at the same time.

"Yes. We've been personally acquainted for years now. I know the shipwright as well."

"You know the shipwright with undeniable skills and who is also an international tradesman?"

"I do."

"Now, I really can't wait to meet them." Gar let out a low whistle, thinking how rich the merchant who owned such an elaborate ship must be. Nobles often looked down upon wealthy tradesmen since they didn't make the supplies they sold. They only profited off of someone else's wares, upping the prices to sell the cargo at trade fairs, pocketing a good amount of money for themselves. "I would love to shake hands with the man who constructed the *Lady Josefina*."

Sage continued, "Bartholomew Woods is the shipwright, but he is no longer in the trade since he is old and his hands cramp up too badly to work anymore."

"What about the merchant, Donald Waterman?"

"He's not old, but he is—"

"Never mind." Gar held up a hand, not wanting to have to receive all his information from a girl. "I'll find out everything for myself. Where is this merchant? I am anxious to set sail."

"As a matter of fact, here comes the merchant now. Shall I introduce you?" asked Sage with a smile.

"Yes, please do." Gar spun around to meet the prosperous man, but couldn't find him anywhere. Instead, he only saw a small woman with flowing, golden-brown tresses. Her small body was covered by a long blue cloak. He looked over her head, still searching for the merchant.

"Where is he, Sage? I don't see him."

"Lord Gar, I'd like to introduce you to Josefina," he heard Sage say, but he wasn't looking at her. Instead, he continued to scan the crowded dock.

"Aye, I'm already familiar with *Josefina*," he answered, glancing back at the ship docked in port. "And damned, she has the right curves and swells that would fire up any man. I can't wait to get my hands on her and take her for a ride."

To his astonishment, the small woman in the long cloak stepped forward, stomping her foot down on his.

"Ow!" he cried out as she quickly stepped backward

again. Anger and confusion clouded his mind. The woman just stood there glaring at him. There was no doubt it wasn't an accident but instead done on purpose. "What the hell are you doing?" he growled. "Don't you know who I am?" he continued, not giving her a chance to answer. "You just assaulted a noble!"

"Excuse me, but I am not inclined to stand here and do nothing while being insulted by someone speaking about my curves and wanting to ride me, no matter if he is a noble or just a waif. I may be a woman, but will not be so disrespected and referred to as naught more than a whore."

Confused and befuddled, Gar found himself speechless. What in God's name was wrong with the wench? And what the hell was she talking about?

"You are obviously addled and completely out of your mind," he ground out, noticing people on the dock watching intently. Gar covered the hilt of his sword with his palm as a subtle reminder to the wench that she not try something so bold again. "I don't even know you. Why do you act as if you think I was speaking about you? I was talking about the ship." He stretched out his arm to show her.

Suddenly, her face reddened and she lowered her gaze to the ground. "I apologize, my lord. I was mistaken and it won't happen again. Please forgive me." She even managed to curtsy, but it didn't make him forgive her and neither did it make him feel any better.

Sage cleared her throat to get Gar's attention. When Gar looked over at her, he swore she was holding back from laughing. "My friend's name is Josefina. That ship was built by her father, Bartholomew Woods, the shipwright. The ship was named after her at her husband's insistence," Sage explained. Suddenly everything became clear.

"I agree with Josefina," interrupted Gar's outspoken cousin, Martine. "You shouldn't talk that way about women. It's not right. Actually, I would have slapped you if I were her." Martine stepped over to put her arm around the girl's shoulders, showing who she supported.

Gar shook his head. "I was talking about the ship and you all know it. Even if I hadn't been, this girl can't get away with stomping on the foot of a noble." Gar was not at all pleased with the situation.

"It was an honest mistake," Eleanor chimed in, walking over and standing on the other side of the woman called Josefina.

"What is going on here?" mumbled Gar, thinking all the women had gone mad.

"If you would have read your orders, I think you'd know," said Rook, slapping the parchment against Gar's chest. "It's all here in plain writing. The merchant, Donald Waterman died six months ago. This is his widow, Josefina. You know, the one the ship was named after."

"Yes. I understand that part now." Gar's attention went back to the girl. "I'm sorry to hear your husband has died, but you can't join me on this journey, if that is your intent."

"Why not?" the feisty wench challenged him. "My husband belonged to the Merchants' Guild. As his widow, it is my right to claim his business and continue to carry it out after his death."

"You. Really? A woman." Gar chuckled lowly and then wished he hadn't. All of the women standing there glared at him now. "I mean... how? How can you carry out his business by yourself?"

"I'm not by myself," she informed him. "Clovis, my brother-by-marriage took over as captain at my husband's death. He has traveled to every port with Donald since the start of his business."

"And where is Clovis now?" asked Gar.

"He's been injured and has a broken leg. That, Lord Gar, is why I needed to hire another captain and why you are even here at all."

"What about his first mate?" asked Gar. "Couldn't he captain the ship?"

"He could." The girl looked down and brushed invisible lint off her shoulder. "But if you must know, I don't trust Hothead Harry at all."

"Hothead Harry?" Gar chuckled at the name. "I can see why. And although you've never met me before now, you trust me? Or is it because you heard the rumors that I'm a pirate and you thought I could ward off danger?"

Her head snapped up and her eyes opened wide. That seemed to alarm her.

"If you must know, I took the word of my good friend, Sage, that you are the man for the job. Plus, your father is the Lord Warden of the Cinque Ports so I thought you could be trusted."

"Did you, now?" he mumbled, finding it ironic that he was losing his job with the king because of being called a pirate, yet this stranger was letting him sail the ship, not afraid that he might steal it along with all the cargo.

"Lord Gar, are you saying you are not trustworthy?"

asked Josefina, squinting one eye and perusing him up and down. "Perhaps I've made a poor decision, after all."

"Nay, Josefina, you didn't," Sage assured her friend. "Gar is just... he's just..."

"Pig-headed, extremely vulgar, demeaning to women, and thinks only about himself," Eleanor finished the sentence for her. "That's my brother to the bone."

"Nay!" Sage's eyes darted first to Gar and then over to her husband. She seemed horrified. "That's not what I meant. Honest, that is not what I was going to say at all."

"Why not?" Robin chuckled. "I have to say that Gar is indeed all those things and more. However, I assure you that he is a trustworthy man," he added in Gar's defense.

"I agree, he is a little odd, but you really have nothing to fear," said Rook. "And don't listen to the wagging tongues because he is not a pirate. Anymore." Rook looked over at Gar and nodded, obviously trying to make up for upsetting him earlier. If he had omitted the "anymore" at the end of his sentence, Gar might have accepted that as an apology.

"I see," said Josefina, blinking several times in succession and then nodding her head. "Good." She cleared her throat. "Well, then I suggest we embark because it is time we leave." She looked over at Sage. "Are you sure you won't join us, Sage?"

"What?" spat Gar. "Nay, she's not going. And neither are you." The last thing he needed or wanted was women on board. Just this one was already proving to be burdensome and he had yet to agree to let her join the voyage.

"I wish I could join you, but I can't," objected Sage, taking Josefina by the hands. "I'm nearly six months pregnant and my husband thinks I'll get seasick on the water. He is probably right. It is better that I keep my feet on land until after the baby is born."

"That's darn right. You're not going anywhere on a ship," Robin commanded. "It's much too dangerous."

"I understand," Josefina answered. "However, I do wish I wasn't the only woman on board."

"Easy," said Gar. "Stay on shore and you won't be the only woman on board."

"That is not what I meant at all," answered Josefina. "Like I already told you, it is time for me to figure out how to handle my late husband's business."

"Wait a minute," said Gar, lifting his hand. "So, are you telling me that this is the first time you'll be handling your husband's affairs?"

"Nay," said the girl. "But I usually travel with others by land and meet them at the ports. On the other hand, this will be the first time I am traveling by ship to the trade fairs and I am very much looking forward to it."

Gar groaned. "Well, that's one of us. You know, it would probably be best for you to just meet the ship at the trade fairs like before. Why change something that you already know works?"

"I can't. There is no time for that." Josefina's face changed and now she held a perturbed expression, if he wasn't mistaken. "The trade fair starts tomorrow. Besides, Clovis promised me I could start traveling by boat with the others."

"Ship," Gar said under his breath, thinking that every woman alive didn't know the difference between a damned boat and a ship. "You do realize that having a woman on board is prohibited and also bad luck."

21

"Is that so?" she said, and seemed to be in deep thought. "I wouldn't want bad luck," said Josefina, making Gar think for a mere second that she would change her mind and be traveling on land instead.

Gar grinned, thinking he'd won. "That's right. We don't want bad luck," repeated Gar, glad that he'd be getting his way after all. Or so he thought. That is, until he heard her next words.

"To avoid bad luck, I prefer another woman to join me on the trip. There is safety in numbers."

"Huh?" Gar felt a sinking sensation in his stomach. This wasn't at all what he wanted.

"I'll go in Sage's place," Martine eagerly volunteered.

"What?" said Gar and Robin at the same time. Rook just watched, but remained silent with a dung-eating grin on his face.

"Sure, why not? It'll be fun." Martine smiled, but Gar frowned even more.

"Oh, would you really travel with me? That would be wonderful. I would love to have you join me," said Josefina excitedly. "But wouldn't it be an inconvenience to you?"

"Yes," said Gar at the same time Martine said "nay."

Martine shot Gar a disgruntled look and continued. "Josefina, I am headed up to Scotland anyway. I am planning to meet up with my cousin, Lady Lark MacKeefe. This will be a much faster way to get there."

"And we can pick you back up after we return from Denmark," added Josefina.

"Yes, that sounds perfect," said Martine as if it were all set.

"Now wait a minute," protested Gar but the women turned giddy after that.

"Oh, Martine, that is a great idea," agreed Eleanor, all but jumping up and down. "I have commitments or I would go too. I am so jealous of you two right now."

"Sister, you are not going on the ship," Robin told Martine in a strict voice. "I won't allow it."

"If Josefina agrees to let me ride along, then I don't see a problem, Robin." Martine sounded as if she really believed that. "After all, it is her ship and she has invited me to travel with her!"

"Yes, I do agree to you joining us, Lady Martine. I do, I do," said Josefina.

"Then it's settled." Sage gave them a satisfied nod. "Have a great trip, you two." The women hugged.

"Nay! Nothing is settled," protested Gar. "I don't want two women aboard, let alone one."

"And I won't let my sister go aboard the ship unescorted," complained Robin. "She is a noblewoman and will be vulnerable and not at all protected from a ship full of lusty men."

"Then why don't you go along to protect her?" suggested Sage. "She'll be safe with a mighty warrior such as yourself at her side, Robin."

"What?" Robin made a sour face. "What are you saying, wife? You really want me to go?"

"Sure. Why not?" asked Sage. "I'll be fine in your absence. I'll be safely tucked away at Saltwood Castle. Besides, you don't have any commitments for the next month and the baby won't be here for several months yet. Go along with them, please. Martine needs you."

"But—" started Robin, but he was cut off by Josefina.

"Aren't you a knight?" she asked.

"Yes. Yes, of course, I am," answered Robin, standing up a bit straighter, his pride taking over now.

"Then, I agree with Sage," continued Josefina. "I'd want no one other than you to protect us on our journey. Lady Martine, please gather your things. We need to set sail anon."

"I'll help you pack," offered Eleanor as the women started away, clucking like hens in Gar's opinion.

"Wait for me," said Sage, giving her husband a quick kiss goodbye. "Have a good time, Robin. I'll see you soon." She hurried off after the other women.

"What just happened?" asked Robin, staring at the backs of the women who walked over the docks arm-in-arm as he rubbed the back of his neck.

"To me, it sounded as if you just agreed to go along to protect the women," said Rook.

"Nay, I didn't." Robin looked over at Gar and grimaced. "Did I?"

"Well, I didn't hear you objecting much," was Gar's response.

"The women tricked us." Robin's eyes flashed over to the backs of the women once more as they hurriedly headed toward a horse and wagon manned by one of the servants, and with a castle guard standing next to it.

"Look, it wasn't my idea to have any of you along on the journey," spat Gar. "Don't worry, I'll put a stop to this." He took a step to go after them.

"No, you won't," said Rook, stopping him in his tracks.

"What do you mean?" asked Gar. "I'm captain and they'll have to follow my orders."

"If you would have taken the time to read your orders, you'd know that Josefina is the one in charge on this journey. You answer to her now until you return from the trade fairs."

"Nay!" Gar laughed. He hurriedly opened the parchment, scanning it frantically, wanting to prove Rook wrong.

"You've got to be jesting," said Robin, with a stiff chuckle. "Aren't you?"

"Nay." Rook shook his head. "The terms are right there and Gar signed the parchment agreeing to them."

"Damn," said Gar, feeling the knot in the pit of his stomach twisting harder now. He regretted having been in such a hurry to sign the papers that he hadn't read them carefully first. Gar had been careless in his excitement to get aboard the *Lady Josefina*. Sure enough, it was all there in writing. It also said he wouldn't be paid until the job was finished. In his eagerness to captain the ship of his dreams, it seems he had sold his soul to the devil without even realizing it. Never would he have willingly agreed to take orders from a woman, or to not get at least half his money upfront. Things were going from bad to worse.

"Pardon me, Lord Gar." A messenger riding a horse with his father's crest on the trappings stopped next to them. "I have a missive from your father." The messenger dismounted and gave the folded parchment to Gar, holding it in two hands and bowing, as was proper.

"Thank you, but when did my father give this to you?"

"Early this morning while everyone slept. I was to find

you when you awoke, but it seems no one knew exactly where you went."

Gar had hurried to the docks first thing this morning, eager to see the ship and he hadn't been back all day.

"Thank you. You're dismissed."

"Thank you, my lord." The messenger left.

"What is it?" asked Robin. "What does your father want?"

"I'm not sure." Gar ran his thumb over the wax seal with the crest of the Lord Warden upon it. Breaking it, he opened the parchment and quickly read what his father had written. "Damn it, you were right, Rook."

"About what?" asked Robin.

"I am guessing you mean about your marriage?" asked Rook.

"Aye." Gar folded up the parchment and shoved it into his pouch along with his orders. "It seems the king has dismissed me from captaining any of his ships until I marry a noblewoman. Only then will he reconsider me for a position again. So, it looks as if this will truly be my last journey on the water unless I find a noblewoman to marry quickly."

"Just marry the first noblewoman you see and you'll be back to sailing ships in no time," suggested Robin.

"It's not that easy," said Gar with a sigh. "My father also says the king feels in order for me to be accepted as a noble and to stop the gossip that I am naught but a pirate, I am to marry, stay on land, and produce an heir within the next year. Only then will he reconsider me worthy of possibly captaining a royal ship in the future."

"A year isn't all that long," said Robin, trying to sound optimistic.

"A year on land and not allowed on the sea is like a life-time sentence to me." Gar felt his heart breaking.

"Aye. That's tough," agreed Rook. "Do you know any noblewomen who'd want to marry you, by any chance?"

Gar looked over to the group of women who just left them, shaking his head. He highly doubted his sister or cousin would want to introduce him to any of their friends. "Nay. Not a one."

"I'll fetch my things and be right back," said Robin as he and Rook walked away discussing the journey.

Gar cast another glance over his shoulder at the ship of his dreams. All his excitement over this journey might have been for naught. He had a feeling gnawing at his insides that before this trip was finished, his dreams would be nothing more than nightmares, after all.

CHAPTER 2

Within the hour, the *Lady Josefina* was loaded. Josefina stood with Lady Martine on deck and at the sidewall as the boarding plank was snatched away and the mooring lines holding the ship to the wharf were tossed. Gulls squawked and circled overhead, looking and hoping for scraps of food. The wind blew strong, the scent of fish heavy in the air.

Looking over the side of the ship and down at the dock, Josefina suddenly felt anxious. The place bustled with people, all going about their business. Fishermen hauled nets and baskets to and from their boats. Merchants selling bread and ale walked up and down the dock, calling out for customers. Wagons clunked over the dock carrying supplies. This was all part of a busy morning. On land, that is. She was about to leave this security behind and head out onto the sea with a ship full of men she barely knew and a captain that already didn't like her. What in the world was she doing?

With no husband at her side, Josefina had bravely taken up his position as an international trade merchant. But now that she was aboard this huge ship with all the crew scurrying around her tending to their chores, she started having second thoughts whether she even wanted to do this at all. Mayhap meeting the new captain at their destination in Scarborough would have been safer for her. It certainly would have been more comforting. But time was running out and she needed to be at the trade fair at the start. Plus, she had to watch over her expensive cargo. The only thing to do now was to make it to her destination quickly. The way to accomplish that was by being on this ship.

"What's the matter?" asked Martine, waving goodbye to Sage and Eleanor standing on the pier. Sage smiled and rubbed her belly with one hand, calling out to them as well as her husband, waving with her other hand high in the air. Eleanor kept her composure and waved like a true lady. Slow, controlled and calculated. They were escorted by one of the castle guards. A servant had come along to drive the wagon. "You looked perplexed, Josefina," said Martine, still smiling and waving to those on shore.

"Nay, all is good. Everything is fine." Josefina flashed a quick smile and tried to look as if she believed what she'd just said. She didn't want anyone, especially the crew, to know just how insecure she felt right now. Not knowing how she was going to make it on her own as a business-woman and no longer having a husband, she was worried beyond belief.

"You miss Donald, don't you?" asked Martine, placing her hand on top of Josefina's on the railing, giving it a light squeeze. "I'm sorry. I know how hard this must be for you, but please don't fret."

"Can I speak freely with you, my lady?" she asked.

"Of course. What it is?" Martine released Josefina's hand and stood up straighter, studying her face in question. "Please, tell me."

"All right, I will." Josefina took a deep breath and released it before continuing. "I know I should be in mourning over the loss of Donald, but I'm not really that saddened by his death at all."

Martine gasped and held her hand to her mouth as if she were horrified to hear this.

"Please, don't think I am cold-blooded and heartless."

"Nay. Of course, not."

"I miss being married more than I do being married to him if that makes any sense at all."

"Why is that?" asked Martine.

"Well, we weren't married that long. Actually, it was only about two years. You see, I don't even feel as if I knew Donald. He was always working and never home. We spent very little time together and never talked unless it was about the business." She watched Martine's expression which didn't change, and realized she shouldn't have said this. She supposed it wasn't making her situation any better. "Oh, nay. Now you think I am haughty and heartless, don't you? Just admit it."

"I didn't say that. Please, Josefina, tell me more. I mean, I thought you must have spent quite a bit of time together to know the trade of being a merchant since there is so much to learn."

"I learned basically everything I know from Clovis, my brother-by-marriage. He is Donald's brother."

"Oh, I see."

"My father and Donald and I lived with Clovis and his wife, Amelia, and their children for many years after my mother passed away."

"I thought your father was a shipwright."

"He was, but since finishing the *Lady Josefina* he hasn't built another ship. He said he is too old to do that kind of work anymore."

"Ladies, we are ready to set sail," came Gar's deep voice from the helm. "Please move toward the aft of the ship and stay out of the way of the crew while they are working."

"Aye, aye, Captain," said Martine, laughing. "My cousin can be so bossy sometimes. I hope he isn't going to be too much for you to accept on this trip."

"Nay," said Josefina, looking up to the handsome man directing the crew from behind the ship's wheel on the sterncastle. "I just hope he doesn't give me trouble since he doesn't seem to like the fact that I am in charge on this journey."

"Martine, Josefina, come away from there until we are out to sea." Robin approached, escorting Martine across the deck and out of the way of the crew. Josefina didn't move.

"Where is my quartermaster?" shouted Gar.

"I'm here, Cap'n," replied the quartermaster, Theobald. He was an older, bald man and was called T-Bald by the crew. T-Bald hurried up the steps of the raised deck to join Gar and get his orders.

"Hoist the main sail," Gar gave the command from the helm.

"Aye, Cap'n," shouted Solomon, the bowman from the deck, directing the crew. He was in charge of the sails and raising and lowering the anchor. Solomon was called Solobow by the others.

The sterncastle was where the captain steered the ship. It was built up high in the air behind the mizzen mast and ran from the main mast all the way to the back of the ship. The forecastle, the deck at the front of the ship, was raised up as well. Josefina knew her father had designed the ship this way to make it harder for seafaring bandits to board. It also gave the crew an advantage if fighting between two vessels should break out. She had been aboard the ship before, but now everything seemed so different. Looking up at the ratlines, she followed the masts up high, all of them stretching so far they seemed to end in the clouds. The ship groaned and creaked as it headed out to sea with waves slapping up against the wooden hull. Her eyes closed momentarily. Her heart raced, thumping against her ribs. The rocking was hard to get used to. Her legs felt like rubber. Josefina would never admit it aloud, but being on a ship at sea scared her. That was the main reason she always traveled over land, meeting the ship at the ports that were not across the channel or wide open expanses of water.

The ship listed to starboard and then back to port, causing Josefina to stumble backward. "Oh!" she cried out, her eyes popping back open to see a blue sky above her. She would have surely fallen down if two strong arms hadn't caught her and pulled her back to an upright position.

"Are you all right?" A man's deep voice was in her ear. When she turned to see who had caught her, her heart beat even faster than before. It was her new sea captain, Lord Gar

Blackmore. With his arms around her, their bodies pressed close together, making their position seem too intimate for being strangers.

"I am fine," she said, noticing the breathiness of her own voice. She raised her gaze to see the handsome man staring down at her. His eyes were brown like the earth, his hair dark like a starless midnight sky. Faint lines creased his forehead, making him seem like a seasoned sailor. Most nobles were pale, as that was sought after. Only commoners and peasants were golden from working in the natural elements. He, on the other hand, had tanned skin, kissed by the sun. A smattering of whiskers trailed from under his nose to below his mouth. His essence was of salt air and leather. Gar Blackmore looked to be a strong, brave man. She liked that. His wide chest and the muscles in his arms reassured her that he was quite capable of the job she'd hired him to do. The crew had to be in good physical condition to be able to pull the ropes to raise the sails, batten down the hatches, or even steer the ship in bad weather. He would also serve as a good protector if she should need one.

"Why didn't you go to the aft of the ship like I instructed?" asked Gar, his voice clipped and irritated.

"I didn't see a need to," she answered, slowly coming back from the dreamy state she was in.

"I gave you a direct order."

"Well, I don't take orders from anyone. You know full well that I am in charge on this journey."

"I see. So, if I want you to remove your hands from my chest so I can get back to the helm, I have to ask?"

"What?" She shook her head, following his gaze downward. Sure enough, she was touching the front of his tunic, even though she hadn't remembered putting her hands there. "Oh!" she cried in horror, pulling away. But when she tried to step back from him, she couldn't move. It was because she was locked tightly in his protective embrace. "Release me at once," she retorted, feeling embarrassed to be in this position, noticing all the men watching them now.

"You're in charge. Whatever you say." He unclasped his arms and turned to go. The ship rocked again, and she had to grab on to a nearby line in order to keep her balance.

"Wait. Where are you going?" she called out to him.

"I have a job to do," he said, starting to climb the steps to the quarterdeck, not even bothering to look back at her. The man had great balance and moved across the deck and up the steps smoothly like a wildcat on the prowl. This setting was natural to him, but to her it was awkward and foreign. "You hired me to sail your ship and that is what I'll be doing. That is, if I stop having so many distractions."

"I want to talk to you, Captain."

"Then come up to the helm. I don't have time to follow you around, catching you each time you stumble, which looks to be about every minute or two. I still don't know why the hell you are even here."

All the pleasure of being in Gar's strong arms fled as soon as he opened his mouth. It only reminded her of what the man's sister had said about him. Lady Eleanor had called him rude, arrogant, and disrespectful to all women. She could see now that it was true. That she wasn't going to be accepted on her ship. Yet, this was her mission. She needed to set him straight before this situation got out of hand. Josefina stormed up the steps after him, not finished with their conversation.

"What's she doing up here? She doesn't belong here." It was Hothead Harry who was Gar's first mate. Josefina never liked the man and felt uncomfortable in his presence.

"I am in charge on this trip, Harry," she told him. "And whether you like it or not, I will go wherever I wish and whenever I want." She turned quickly to talk to Gar, and her stomach lurched. It was so high up on the quarterdeck that it almost made her feel dizzy. She didn't like it up here at all.

"Harry, man the helm. I'm going to take Josefina down to the cabin and get her out of the way once and for all." Gar took a hold of her arm and started walking down the stairs, nearly dragging her behind him.

As much as Josefina wanted to prove her point, she didn't object to getting off the high quarterdeck first. The ship was barely out of port and already she felt as if she were going to be sick.

"Come along," he said, holding her arm tightly, taking her with him as he descended the stairs and hurried over to the captain's quarters below the sterncastle. "It is more than evident you have never sailed before."

"That's not true," she protested. "I have sailed many times. Just not on a boat as big as this one."

"Ship," she heard him say under his breath. He opened the door to the cabin, gently guiding her inside where she found Martine looking out the small round window at the sea. Robin sat on a chair with his arms folded over his chest and his feet up on a small bed.

"Ah, there you are," said Robin, doing nothing to even get up off his bottom end to greet them.

"Josefina, where were you?" Martine rushed over, seeming to have no trouble at all at keeping her balance as the ship rocked back and forth. "I thought you were right behind us, but when we got to the cabin, I realized you were gone."

"I stayed to talk with Lord Gar," she told her new friend.

"Robin, I thought you were going to watch over the girls," grumbled Gar. "I can't sail the ship and keep her from falling at the same time." He dropped her arm. Josefina gladly sat down on the bed.

"I am here to watch over my sister, not both of them," said Robin with a yawn.

"I don't need protecting. Just go back to work." Josefina waved her hand through the air, trying to urge Gar to leave.

"I'll gladly do just that. Now stay in the cabin before you end up falling overboard."

"I am not going to stay inside the cabin for the entire trip," she protested.

"It's not going to be that long. We'll be in Scarborough by tomorrow," Gar explained.

"Gar, you're being unkind and unreasonable," scolded Martine. "Besides, are you forgetting that you take orders from Josefina on this trip?"

"How could I forget?" was his answer. "Robin, watch over them. I've got a crew to instruct." Gar headed for the door.

"Wait," said Robin. "Gar, where are we all going to sleep tonight? This cabin only has two small beds."

"Josefina and I will sleep here while you two sleep out on the deck," said Martine.

"Like hell if I'm going to do that," snapped Gar. "After all, I'm the captain. I'll need my rest when it is not my shift."

"Gar, I didn't come along on the journey to sleep out on the deck with that questionable crew," complained Robin. "I'll take one of the beds."

"Questionable crew?" repeated Josefina. "Lord Robin, are you saying there is something wrong with my crew?" They weren't the best nor the most trustworthy, but Josefina didn't want the man insulting her crew.

"I have to admit, a few of them look more like pirates than the pirates I once knew," admitted Gar.

"Like who?" asked Josefina crossing her arms over her chest.

"How about Hothead Harry and Two Spit Sam for starters?" asked Gar. "I really wish I'd been able to choose my own crew for this journey. I promise, they would have been better than this one that was chosen for me."

"The crew will be fine, Lord Gar," she told him, just wanting him to shut up. "And, Lord Robin, you can't expect me and Martine to sleep out on the deck with the men."

"Nay, of course, not," said Robin with a shrug. "But Gar and I are nobles. You can't expect us to sleep on the deck either."

"I don't see any other choice," said Josefina.

"I suppose we can all share the cabin then," continued Robin, not about to agree with her. "It'll be cozy and my cousin snores, but I'm game."

"I do not snore," said Gar. "Or not much, anyway."

"Gar, I am related to the two of you so it doesn't matter, but you can't expect Josefina to share a room with two men who are strangers to her," said Martine.

"Then, we'll let Josefina decide where we will all sleep, since she is making the decisions," said Gar, looking directly into Josefina's eyes, causing a hot shiver to run through her. "But just let me make one thing clear. It is bad enough that the crew already knows I have been tricked into taking orders from a woman. If they see the captain getting kicked out of his own cabin, I guarantee you that there will be a mutiny on this ship before the journey is over. That isn't what you want, is it, Josefina?"

"Well, no. Of course, not," she said, feeling the heat rising to her cheeks.

"Josefina?" asked Martine. "Are you saying you want the men to share this cabin with us? I am all right with the decision, but it is up to you."

"I... suppose it will be all right," Josefina softly answered, not able to look directly at Gar when she said it. "I really wouldn't want a mutiny on my ship. It is crucial I get the wares to the trade fair in time. I don't want any trouble."

"Well, then. I'm glad that is settled," said Gar with a quick nod. "Now, I'll be off to the helm. Perhaps you ladies can find some food for us because I am famished." Gar quickly turned and walked out the door.

"Me too," said Robin.

"I have a cook for that," sputtered Josefina, wanting to follow Gar and tell him how disrespectful that statement was. But she was afraid if she ended up in his arms again or looking deeply into his eyes he'd see her blushing. Nay, mayhap it would be better if she just stayed far away from him from now on.

"Robin, I need you on the deck," came Gar's voice from outside the door.

"Aye, Captain," said Robin, standing up and stretching. "Ladies, stay here until I return." With that, he left the room and closed the door.

CHAPTER 3

Gar headed back out to the main deck, stopping for a moment to lean his elbows on the sidewall, staring out to sea. It was a beautiful day without a cloud in the sky. The water was pristine blue and calmer than usual. The large square sails of the main mast and the foremast billowed with air while the lateen or triangular sail on the mizzenmast was mounted on the yardarm on an angle, running in a fore and aft direction.

"Gar, what is it?" asked Robin, coming to join him at the rail. The crew did their jobs without being told and that alone impressed Gar. Yet, there was something that was bothering him.

He looked back and forth and when no one was listening, leaned in to speak in private with his cousin.

"I have a bad feeling about this trip," he told Robin.

"You do? Why? Is it because of the girls?" asked Robin. "I know it is superstition that women on board are bad luck, but do you really believe that to be true?"

"That is just more fuel to add to the fire," Gar answered. "However, it is the crew that worries me more."

"How so?" Robin leaned his back against the rail with his arms out, looking over at the crew. There were thirty men aboard the ship besides Gar, Robin and the girls. They were all scruffy-looking and didn't smile much, but then again they were sea-dwelling men and not expected to be pleasant.

"I don't trust them."

"Gar, you're only going to be with them for a few days. Why should that even worry you? They all look fine to me. Besides, we'll be keeping a close eye on them."

"Most of them cannot look me in the eye," Gar told him.

"They're probably just focusing on their work."

"Mayhap," said Gar, clasping and unclasping his hands together, still staring out to sea. "Then again, mayhap not. I want you to keep an open ear and eye on the crew at all times. If anything seems suspicious, notify me at once."

"Me?" Robin stood up and thumped his hand against his chest. "I'm a knight, unless you've forgotten. A knight who shouldn't be on a ship watching over two addled women to begin with. I should be on the tiltyard practicing the joust or engaging in swordplay with the other knights. Or how about being home with my pregnant wife? I mean, now you want me to spy on the crew as well?"

"Nay. You're right," said Gar, standing up straight. "I suppose I'm just being overly cautious. But I swear something seems off, although I cannot put my finger on what it is."

"I'll do what I can, Gar, but you're asking a lot of me." Robin made his feelings known and Gar supposed he

RIDING OUT THE STORM

couldn't blame him. It was a sacrifice for him to be here at all.

"When we get to Scarborough, secure a room at the inn for yourself and another for the girls."

"What about you?" asked Robin. "Won't you be joining us?"

"I've decided to sleep on this ship. If something deceitful is going on, which my gut tells me is true, then I'll take care of the matter before it gets out of hand."

"All right," said Robin with a careless shrug. "But tell me, are we really sleeping in the cabin with the girls tonight?"

"Why do you even ask? You heard Josefina's decision. Don't you trust yourself around her?" asked Gar.

"Stop it, Gar. I'm a married man now and about to be a father. I'd never stray from Sage and you know it. I was talking about you!"

"What about me?"

"I know how you are around women. Can you trust yourself to keep your hands off of the wench?"

Gar thought about it for a moment. With his arms around Josefina earlier, he had to stop himself from reaching down and kissing her cute little pouty lips. When she gave orders, although it aggravated him, it made her seem more desirable for some reason. He supposed it was the sense of power he was attracted to, not necessarily the girl herself. Her hair cascaded down around her shoulders like a water-fall, but her eyes— those damned beautiful eyes drew him in, making him want to get to know her better. Dammit, why did she have to be so pretty? He wanted to despise her since he was taking orders from her now, but for some reason he couldn't do it.

"I have to find a noblewoman to marry," he told his cousin.

"That's not what I asked. We're talking about the merchant girl."

"I'm not interested in commoners like you or Rook married. I, for one, am going to find someone of my own status. I'll marry a noblewoman and be respected and accepted by not only the king, but everyone. Just the way it should be."

"So, in other words, you'll use the girl for your own needs until you find a noble to take the bait and marry you."

"You make that sound like a bad thing."

"Remember, Josefina is good friends with Sage, and now Martine too. Don't you dare do anything to hurt the girl."

"Hurt her? Hah! We are here to protect the girls. Remember?"

"That's not what I meant and you know it, Gar. Don't break her heart whatever you do. If so, I'll never hear the end of it and I'll be the one to pay, not you."

"Just forget about the girls and keep an eye on the men for now. I'm going back up to take the helm and sail the only lady I truly have eyes for— the *Lady Josefina*."

Josefina spent most of the day working with Martine to hang blankets up in the cabin, partitioning off one side of the room from the other. "There, that should do it," she said, brushing her hands together. "Now, just help me move the other bed to our side of the blanket wall so we don't end up sleeping on the floor. We'll let the men stay there."

They tried to do it, but the bed was bolted to the floor. It was made this way so it wouldn't move whenever the ship rocked back and forth.

"It's not going to work," said Martine.

"I forgot about that. My father made sure none of the furniture would move when he built this ship. Nay, it won't work. Plus, it won't fit on our side of the wall anyway," she answered with a sigh.

There came a knock at the door. Martine hurried over to open it. "Yes?" she asked.

Josefina walked up behind her to see the cabin boy who was sixteen years of age, having worked for her husband since he was just a child. "What is it, Cup?" she asked him.

"Cup?" Martine smiled and looked at her oddly.

"My name is really Cyprian, my lady," said the boy with a bow. "But since none of the crew can ever remember my name they just all call me Cup."

"I don't understand." Martine seemed totally confused.

"He fills the crew's cups at mealtime," Josefina explained. "So, they just hold out their vessels and call for Cup if they want more wine or ale."

"Oh, I see now," Martine answered.

"What is it, Cup?" asked Josefina once again.

The blond-haired boy was thin and lanky, but tall for his age. He wore tattered clothes and had no shoes. His front tooth was chipped and his ears seemed too big for his head. Still, he was charming in his own way.

"The Captain sent me to fetch you," Cup answered. "He says Whiney Wilkens is complaining that the men want to eat but Captain Blackmore said the ladies have to eat first so they have to wait."

"Oh, of course," said Josefina. "Let's not keep them waiting, Lady Martine. Wilkens will always find something to gripe about and I don't want it to be us."

"My, the crew has some odd names," said Martine, following Josefina out the door.

"Stay away from Two Spit Sam when he's eatin' fish," warned the boy. "He likes to spit the bones out and doesn't care who he hits. Especially when he's just hocking up phlegm."

"I'll keep that in mind, thank you," said Martine.

"And if Crusty Rusty starts dancin' around, it means he's drunk so run the other way," continued the boy. "He picked me up and put me over his shoulder once and would have thrown me over the sidewall if I hadn't managed to get away and climb up to the lookout basket."

"He did what?" asked Martine in surprise.

"He won't follow me up there because his legs are bowed and he has a hard time goin' higher than halfway without fallin'. Well, at least when he's well in his cups," said the boy. Then a wide grin crossed his face. "I'm also much faster than him so he can't catch me. Sometimes some of the crew pay me to taunt the man just to see his face get red."

"My, that is an odd thing to do." Martine obviously wasn't used to being around men like this. She seemed unsettled by what Cup was telling her.

"Thank you, Cup. We'll keep all that in mind. That's enough for now," said Josefina, getting to the main deck to see the entire crew standing around glaring at her. With their arms crossed over their chests, they looked hungry enough to kill.

"This way, ladies," said Robin, walking over and directing them to a wide board set up over some barrels. Four more barrels were placed around the make-shift table for Gar, Robin, Martine and Josefina to sit on while they ate. "Well, this is cozy," said Martine, letting Robin help her seat herself atop a barrel. Martine was an unusual noble-woman, thought Josefina. Nothing much seemed to bother her. "I can't wait to see what we have to eat."

Two Spit groaned. Some of the other crew spoke softly to each other. Josefina heard them complaining that there might not be enough for them now that the women were here.

"Martine, you always sound so optimistic. Are you always that way?" asked Josefina, taking a seat next to Martine before Robin could assist her. Gar was still up at the helm with T-Bald.

"My sister, optimistic? Hah!" said Robin, looking thoroughly amused.

"Robin," scolded Martine under her breath. "Be nice."

"All I can say is that Martine used to be quite haughty and very judgmental," Robin told Josefina, taking a seat at the table across from Martine. "We never got along and were always at odds with each other, growing up."

"Really?" asked Josefina in surprise. "Do you come from a large family?"

"Not really," said Robin. "I'm the oldest, then Martine, and we have two younger sisters."

"Ah, you're the only boy," said Josefina with a nod, understanding the situation.

"Yes, but I always got along with our sisters, Regina and Dorothy. It was just Martine and I who quarreled."

"Mayhap so, but it's not like that anymore." Martine looked down and brushed some dirt off the board that served as their table.

"It's true what she says," agreed Robin. "After she met Sage, things changed. I think my wife showed her a different way of life." Robin nodded, seeming satisfied. "Sage is a wonderful woman who can change anyone just by her words and kindness."

"Mayhap, Brother, it was you who Sage changed for the better, not me," protested Martine. Cup approached with a bottle of wine and poured some into Martine's wooden cup. Then the boy poured some for Josefina as well.

"Thank you, Cyprian," said Josefina, smiling warmly at the boy.

"What did she say?" asked Crusty Rusty, from a distance, lifting a side of his mouth as he spoke. His red hair stuck out in all directions. The man always had a look on his face like he smelled spoiled fish. Plus, he often squinted one eye when he spoke.

"I think she's talkin' about her wine," said Solobow. He was taller than most of the crew, and very skinny. His knees and elbows were knobby.

"Nay, she's not. She's talkin' about the runt." Two Spit Sam's tongue shot out and he turned his head and spat on the deck, hitting Whiney Wilken's leg with his spittle.

"You cur! I just washed my trews." Whiney shook his leg. "Just for that, you don't get any of my pork and lentil pottage."

"Just try to keep it from me and see what happens, you whiner." Two Spit stuck his face up to Whiney and growled like a bear.

"Enough!" Gar handed over the helm to his quarter-master and hurried down the steps to stop a fight that was about to break out. "Cook, serve the table and then the rest of you can eat."

"Why do we even have the women on board?" asked Hothead, pushing his way to the front of the line as Whiney and Cup served the nobles and Josefina their meals first. "They'll bring us bad luck, I tell ye. We should dump them when we get to Scarborough and travel on to Scotland without them."

"Harry, I don't want to hear another complaint from you about the women. Do you understand?" Gar needed to keep control of the crew and ship before something happened to the women.

Harry scoffed and whispered something to Two Spit. Gar didn't like this in the least. He walked up and grabbed Hothead Harry by the front of his tunic, gripping him tightly. In a firm voice and glaring at the man, he continued. "I said, do you understand?" he asked again in a deep growl.

"Savvy, Cap'n," said Hothead, scowling and looking the other way.

Gar let him go before joining the others at the plank table. He sat down, feeling uncomfortable. When the man said 'savvy' it brought back a flash of memory from when Gar was raised with pirates. Immediately, his memories took him back to a time that he'd tried hard to forget. He was only four years old, but remembered his life back then as if it had happened just yesterday.

Gar's mother, Echo, had been raised by a man called Captain Powell ap Llyr, one of the meanest pirates of the North Sea. Still, he was Gar's grandfather. Or so he had thought at the time. That was before his mother's true story had been discovered, how she was really a noble, and stolen as a baby.

Gar hadn't been brought aboard the pirate ship, *The Seahawk,* more than a few times, and only when it was docked. As a young boy, Gar had been fascinated by the ship and wanted more than anything to sail the seas like his mother and grandfather. Instead, his mother always left him behind on land with one of the captain's whores. Gar lived in a dark room above a filthy tavern in Great Yarmouth, seeing and hearing things that no four-year-old should ever be privy to experiencing. Until his mother married his uncle, Garrett Blackmore, and they moved to his manor house, Gar had nightmares frequently, thinking he was abandoned and would never see his mother again. He longed to know his true father, Sir Edgar Blackmore as well, but sadly he never would since he'd been killed by pirates. Being on a ship and on the sea somehow seemed to bring Gar closer to the father he never knew. After all, on the water is where his father lost his life and was buried at the bottom of the sea.

"All right, Wilkens, give the rest of the crew their food now," Gar instructed the cook after those sitting at the table had been served.

"Line up," called out Whiney Wilkens, almost getting trampled as the men each grabbed a square wooden bowl and pushed to get to the front of the line. The bowls were square instead of round, keeping them from rolling if they should be dropped on deck.

"Stop the pushin' and calm down," shouted Whiney as he and Cup dished out the food for the crew. "If I drop this, there's not goin' to be food for anyone."

"Damn it, why can't this crew listen?" Gar was on his feet, meaning to put them all in line, but Josefina shot up from the table and darted in front of him.

"I'll handle them," she said, rushing past him and over to the men. She said something to them and like magic, the men all got back into one line and stopped their pushing.

"How did she do that?" asked Gar, impressed and a little jealous that a woman could do something that he could not. He hurried after her, stopping in his tracks when he saw her handing a coin to each man standing still in line. "What the hell are you doing?" he asked, coming to her side.

"Josefina is giving each of us a ha'penny to stand quiet and still in the food line," said one crewmember, holding out his open palm. Josefina, dropped a halfpenny into it.

"Nay, she's not." Gar snatched the bag of coins away from her, getting nothing but complaints from the men.

"Give it back," she demanded. Her angry eyes bore into him.

"You cannot bribe these men to listen to you," he told her, pulling her away from the line of men.

"Why not? It's not much money, and at least they listen to me."

That comment hurt. Gar didn't want to fight in front of the men, and neither did he want the men to see the way the girl challenged him. It wasn't proper. Especially, not for a woman to do so.

"Come with me." He didn't give her a chance to object. He grabbed her by the arm and hauled her across the deck.

"What about my ha'penny?" complained Two Spit.

"I didn't get one either," said another man.

"Anyone who thinks they are being treated unfairly can

meet with me personally." Gar drew his sword and held it up. "But I will warn you that you won't win against my sword."

"Lord Gar! Really!" Josefina's eyes opened wide. "Are you saying you are going to kill the men if they think they've been treated unfairly?"

"Why not?" asked Hothead. "After all, he's a pirate and that's what pirates do."

Gar let go of Josefina so fast that she almost fell. He reached out, pulling Hothead Harry to him, his blade resting against the man's neck. Anger filled Gar. It took all his willpower not to slit the man's throat for what he'd said.

"This proves my point," Harry yelled out to the others. Suddenly, everyone was quiet and the only sound was the splashing of the waves against the sidewall of the ship. Gar looked from one man to the next, feeling like that pirate of a grandfather, not wanting to be this way. When he glanced over to Robin and Martine, they were shaking their heads and looking sorely disappointed in him.

"Damn it, get your food and get back to your posts. All of you," he commanded, sheathing his sword.

"Well, that didn't work so well, did it?" asked the smart-mouthed Josefina.

"I may be finished with the crew, but I'm far from done with you." He took her arm and pulled her into the captain's cabin, closing the door behind him.

Josefina quickly stepped away from Gar, not liking the way he'd just acted on deck. She agreed with the crew that he was coming across as being a pirate, but she didn't dare tell him. If she did that, he might kill her right here in the cabin with no one to stop him.

"Why are you looking at me like that?" he asked, walking toward her like a wild animal stalking its prey. She continued to back up across the room, not wanting to be close to him right now.

"Like what?" she asked, faking a quick smile. She saw him frown. His dark eyes were locked on her, making her feel as if she could no longer move.

"You think I'm a pirate too. Just like the rest of the men do. Don't you?"

"Nay. I didn't say that. I don't think that at all."

"Then why do you look frightened of me?" He stopped right in front of her now. He was so close that their toes nearly touched.

"You can't blame a woman for feeling frightened of someone who is so big and strong and..." She swallowed forcefully when he reached out and cupped her cheek with his large palm.

Then, he spoke to her in a soft voice. "I'm sorry if I frightened you, Josefina. That was not my intent at all." His gaze flitted down to her mouth. He stood so close to her that she swore she could feel the heat from his body. Or was it her body heat she was experiencing? "I was only trying to protect a beautiful young woman from being taken advantage of by the scurvy dogs of this crew. You can't let them control you. And you are so easy to control."

"I can't be controlled," she said in a breathy whisper, feeling her body heat up even more when his thumb stroked across her bottom lip. Damn, why couldn't she push him away? Instead, her eyes closed and she let him do it. She oddly liked being touched by such a rugged, strong man. Something about it excited her, though she didn't want to like this man at all. "However, you need to remember that I give the orders on this journey. It is right in our contract." Her eyes opened and her heart beat faster to see what was about to happen.

"Of course. You are in charge," he said, lowering his mouth to hers. He spoke against her lips and she could feel the vibration of his words. And when his lips touched hers in a sensual kiss, her eyes closed again and her head fell back. His arms encircled her. His kiss deepened. It felt so good that she didn't want this to ever end.

But then, he suddenly released her, letting her fall upon the bed. Her eyes snapped open in surprise. "Why did you do that?" she asked, feeling shaken.

"That, my dear, was a little lesson for you." He pulled her back up to her feet.

"What does that mean?" Embarrassed by the way she'd reacted, she straightened out her gown, unable to look directly at him right now.

"I only kissed you to show you how easily a man can control you even when you think you are the one in charge."

"What?" Her heart dropped in her chest. Had he really only pretended to like her and had he only kissed her because it was naught but a stupid lesson?

"I admit, you were easier to control than I had originally thought." He chuckled lowly. "But that is proof that this crew will take from you whatever they can get. So don't think they are listening to you, and God's eyes, don't think they will ever respect you. Remember, you are a female on a ship of men and you don't belong here. They will never let you forget it."

"Well, let me give you something you'll never forget as

well." She reached out and slapped him hard across his cheek, surprising him and sending him stumbling backward a few steps.

"You just slapped a noble?" His hand went to his cheek.

"You are damned right about that," she said, pushing past him and ripping open the door. "And if you ever try such a stunt again, next time it'll be a kick to the groin that you won't be able to forget for months."

Josefina left the cabin and slammed the door behind her.

CHAPTER 4

"**G**ar? Aren't you going to sleep? It's late," said Robin, making his way up to the sterncastle later that night. "Most everyone already retired for the night. Solobow dropped anchor so we won't drift."

"I know. I am just taking first watch." Gar leaned his elbows on the siderail of the raised platform, staring out at the night sky with a bottle of whisky in his hand.

"Surely, you can get Harry or T-Bald to take watch," Robin suggested.

"I can, but I won't."

"Why the hell not?"

"I don't want to go back to the cabin. Not after the way I acted with Josefina."

"Oh, you're worried about Josefina being angry with you for telling her not to give the men money?" Robin leaned on the rail next to Gar, staring out at the night sky as well. The clouds were starting to cover the moon, but bright stars could still be seen dotting the sky.

"That's not it," Gar admitted, really needing to confide in someone about what he was feeling. His only concern was that he wasn't sure Robin would understand. He took another swig from the bottle and shook his head. "Oh, never mind."

"Cousin, I'm here for you. Spill your guts. What has you so upset that it's caused you to give up sleep and end up far in your cups on only the first night of the journey?" He pulled the bottle away from Gar and took a swig. He followed it by releasing a satisfied puff of air from his mouth.

"I pulled my sword and threatened the crew." Gar stared up at the sky when he said it.

"Aye. And because of it, they called you a pirate and now you're upset." Robin took another swig of whisky.

"That's not the part bothering me the most." He yanked the bottle away from Robin. "I mean, I did act like a pirate and I hate myself for that. But I did something worse with Josefina inside the cabin."

"You did?" Robin's eyes opened wide and he chuckled. "You bedded the girl, didn't you? You lucky dog. Josefina is a real looker."

"Nay, I didn't bed her. And yes, she is beautiful. So much so, that when I'm around her, I just can't think straight."

"So, what are you saying?"

"I'm saying I kissed her."

"Oh. That's all?" Robin almost sounded disappointed that there wasn't more to tell. "Well, there is no harm in that."

"There is, because I only did it to teach her a lesson. And

that, dear cousin, is something no better than what a pirate would do." He took another swig of whisky.

"How did she react?" asked Robin.

"She slapped me."

Robin chuckled again. "She is a feisty one, that's for sure. I'm sure she'll never let you get that close to her ever again."

"That's what I'm afraid of."

"How so?"

"She liked the kiss, I know she did. I liked it too," admitted Gar. "And now that I've tasted her sweet lips against mine, I want more. I want to kiss her and make love to her the way she deserves. Not because it's a lesson, but because I oddly have feelings for Josefina even though I just met her."

"Ah, I see," said Robin with a nod. "You are falling fast. And because of your little lesson, Josefina will hate you from now on. What a situation to be in."

"I'm afraid that's true and I don't know what to do."

"Did you try apologizing?"

"I think so." He dragged a hand through his long hair. "Mayhap," he said, followed by a pause. "Oh, hell, perhaps not. I'm not sure. All I know is that now Josefina is convinced I am nothing but a pirate. I will have no chance with her anymore."

"Mayhap it's for the best," said Robin. "I mean, the king ordered you to marry a noblewoman, and you need to follow his command. Even though Josefina has money, a business, and the ship of your dreams, don't forget that she is not noble. Mayhap it is best if you just forget about any feelings you have for her and focus on the job you've been hired to do."

"You're right," said Gar, yawning, handing the bottle to Robin. "Here, take this. It's your watch. I'm going to get some shut-eye."

"My watch? Nay. That is not why I'm here and you know it."

"There are only two beds in that cabin and a blanket wall between them, and you know it," Gar reminded him. "I'm sure the girls are both smashed into one bed, so the other will be mine." He started to descend the steps.

"I didn't come up here to take watch or to give up my bed," said Robin from the sterncastle. "Besides, there is something I need to tell you."

"Whatever it is, it can wait until morning. Now, don't leave the ship unattended," Gar told him, yawning again, feeling a little light-headed from drinking so much. He pushed open the cabin door and stood there in the dark, not able to see a blasted thing.

Josefina lay asleep in one bed, while Martine slept in the bed behind the curtain. Robin left the cabin to tell Gar the sleeping arrangements that were Josefina's orders. She instructed him to let Gar know that the two of them would need to sleep on the deck with the crew instead of inside the cabin. She'd decided this would probably be the best arrangement. After all, men sleeping in the same cabin with women would only cause tongues to wag and she couldn't have that.

She awoke, hearing a noise. When she turned over, she saw a man's silhouette in the moonlight, standing just inside the cabin. He was a big man and wavered back and forth. She was about to cry out, thinking it was one of the crew. Then, when the man turned to close the door, she saw his face. It was Gar. He unclasped his weapon belt and placed it on the table. Next, he quickly kicked off his boots. The room now stank of whisky. She realized he'd been drinking and was probably drunk.

Just as she opened her mouth to tell him he had to leave, he whipped off his tunic and flung it at the bed, hitting her in the face. The moonlight from the lone round window in the cabin snuck through the small opening in the curtain and settled on his broad chest. What she saw caused her to gasp. His bare chest was covered with dark hair that trailed all the way down to the top of his trews. The solidness of his chest and his large biceps looked so amazing that she found herself wanting to reach out and touch him. Shaking her head, she tried to clear her ridiculous thoughts. She needed to remember that this was the man who'd made a fool out of her.

Josefina reached under her pillow for her dagger, wanting to throw it at him to scare him. But when she looked back up, he stood there stark naked, walking toward the bed. All she could do was take a good, long look at God's wonderful work of art.

"God's eyes," she whispered, letting her gaze travel down past his waist and to his manhood. He had quite a male presence, making her squirm on the bed.

"Josefina? Is that you?" He took another wavering step toward her, seeming as if he were having a hard time keeping his balance. And when he got up to the bed, the ship leaned. He lost his balance and stumbled, falling onto the bed along with her. "Sleep, I need sleep," she heard him mumble, rolling toward her. His arm flipped out, landing around her waist. Then one heavy leg did the same to her legs as he hugged her tightly to his body.

Josefina's fingers released the dagger. Panicked, she tried to push out of his hold but he was too strong for her. She was trapped beneath him with no way to release herself from his embrace.

"Let me go. Get away from me," she warned him, not wanting to speak too loudly or she'd waken Martine from the other side of the hanging blanket. What would the noblewoman think of her if she found her in bed with a naked man? Josefina only wore her thin shift, so this wouldn't look innocent in the least. "Gar, wake up," she spat, digging her fingernails into his arm, still trapped under the weight of his heavy body.

"I'll protect you, my raving beauty," he mumbled, kissing her atop the head. And then, just when she didn't think things could get any worse, he started snoring.

Bid the devil! She was pressed up against a naked man in bed and she was barely wearing anything at all. This had to be the worst possible situation ever.

Or so she thought, until she felt his aroused form pressing up against her. Meaning to teach him a lesson, the way he did to her, she reached down between them and grabbed his hardened form and squeezed.

"Oooooh," she said, knowing she'd made a mistake when she felt his hot manhood in her hand. A tingling sensation ran between her legs at the feel of silk over steel. With her fingers wrapped around his erection, his manhood continued to grow and harden. Her body sprang to life with excitement. Josefina wanted this man in every way. "Nay," she said, feeling her heart lodge in her throat. She cursed herself for her wanton actions. Releasing him, she quickly pulled back her hand. When she moved, he smiled in his sleep and moaned. Then he moved his arm. His hand settled over one swell of her breasts and he gave her a squeeze, causing her body to jerk. Damn, it felt good, even if he was drunk and half-asleep and didn't realize what he was doing. She slowly looked down to his hand covering her breast right over her shift. This man was touching her intimately. Where would this lead before the night ended?

And with his hand clamped over her breast and still trapping her there, he started to snore again. Josefina realized that this was now the worst possible thing that could happen to her. Knowing she wasn't going anywhere until Gar awoke, she put her hand over his and closed her eyes hoping to hell she'd be able to sleep because this couldn't really be happening. It had to be naught but a dream.

CHAPTER 5

"Oh, my goodness!" came a woman's voice, waking Gar up from his sleep. He'd been dreaming about Josefina all night long. In his dreams he'd cupped her breast and she'd fondled his hardened manhood. Her skin felt so soft and she smelled so good. He never wanted the feeling to end.

Gar flipped over onto his back and opened his eyes. There stood Martine, fully dressed, staring down at him with her mouth wide open.

"What are you doing, Cousin? You shouldn't be in here, and certainly not naked and like that!" Martine held her hand up to block her eyes, looking the other way. "Where is Josefina?"

"J-Josefina?" he asked. Hearing the girl's name only excited him more. He looked down to his waist. He was covered slightly with the sheet but couldn't contain his erotic thoughts about Josefina. The sheet rose up like a tent.

"Damn it," he ground out, knowing now what Martine was talking about. "Toss me my clothes," he told her.

"Gladly," she said, grabbing his trews from the back of the chair and throwing them to him, still not looking.

Gar stood up and quickly pulled them into place, looking back at the bed, half-expecting Josefina to be there for some reason. Instead, he found it empty, along with his tunic. Damn, his dreams were so real that it was getting hard to tell the difference between the dream world and the waking one. He pulled his crumpled tunic over his head.

"Where are Robin and Josefina?" asked Martine, looking over her shoulder and turning around to face him when she realized he was dressed.

"How the hell should I know?" He grabbed his boots and sank back down on the bed to put them on.

"When I went to sleep last night, Josefina was in that bed. And I wake up to find you." She looked at him suspiciously.

"Well, if you're suggesting anything happened between us, you're wrong," he assured her, standing up and donning his weapon belt. Josefina hates me. I'm sure she told you that."

"Nay, she didn't."

"Then she didn't tell you anything about— I mean, about me?"

"Gar, I have no idea what you are talking about. If you believe Josefina is talking about you, you're wrong, because she isn't."

"Oh," he said, scratching the back of his neck, feeling slightly disappointed. He had been sure she liked the kiss between them as much as he had. If so, why hadn't she even mentioned it to Martine? Isn't that what women usually talk about?

The door to the cabin opened. Robin stood there looking tired as all hell. "Good, you're up," said Robin. "T-Bald took the helm a few hours ago. He said we should reach Scarborough within the hour."

"We're moving? When the hell did we raise anchor? I didn't give the command," snapped Gar.

"Nay, you didn't. You were sleeping. Josefina did," said Robin with a yawn.

"And you let her do it?" This was driving Gar crazy.

"We all know she's in charge, so what is the problem, Cousin?"

"The problem is... the problem is... oh never mind. Get out of my way, I have a ship to run."

"And I have a bed waiting for me." Robin eyed the bed with longing. Gar let him go, realizing he'd been up most of the night.

"I'll be at the helm," Gar announced and hurried out the door.

"I'm coming with you." Martine picked up the hem of her skirt and hurried after him. "I still want to know where Josefina disappeared to."

"We will be approaching Scarborough within the hour," came Josefina's voice from the helm. Gar spun around to see her standing next to T-Bald, shouting so the crew could hear her. He half expected to see her steering the ship as well. He wouldn't have been surprised if she had tried to do it. Josefina was fully dressed and looked nothing like the way he'd seen her in his dreams. "Man the lines and be prepared to move the cargo as soon as we dock." Gar headed up the steps and she saw him. "And give Captain Blackmore plenty of room since he is still well in his cups from last night," she yelled to the crew. "If you get in his way, he may trap you with his large body."

"What are you doing?" He stomped over and took the helm from T-Bald. "You can go now," he told the old man.

"What am *I* doing?" she asked. "I could say the same for you. After all, I am not the one sleeping all morning after having had too much to drink last night."

"How do you know I had too much to drink?" he asked, steering the ship, liking the cool bite of the breeze against his face. "Did you see me last night?" He looked at her from the corners of his eyes as he waited for his answer. This would tell him if what he'd experienced was real or just a dream.

She bit her lip and looked the other way. "Why would I?"

"I was sleeping in the cabin. Weren't you there too?" He was sure she was, or mayhap his dream was so real that he'd only imagined the whole damned thing."

"I have no time for small talk, Captain. I am going to the hold to check the cargo to make sure nothing has been damaged."

"Josefina, there you are." Martine finally made it to the top of the steps. "I went to sleep and you were in the bed but when I woke up, Gar was there instead."

"So... Josefina wasn't sleeping behind the curtain with you?" Gar asked Martine.

"Nay, of course not." Martine made a face.

His head snapped around to Josefina. Her face was red. Was it from the wind and sun, or could it possibly be from embarrassment? And if that were so, had she really been in bed with him like he'd thought? It must be so since she wasn't denying it. A wave of relief shot through him. So, it wasn't a dream, after all.

"Excuse me, I need to check the cargo." Josefina hurried away.

"Wait!" he called out. "I need to speak to you."

"I'm busy," she said, obviously not wanting to talk to him. He couldn't go after her because he was manning the helm. Plus, he didn't want to leave Martine unescorted since Robin was in the cabin sleeping now.

"What's the matter?" asked Martine. "You seem so distraught."

"That girl is going to be the end of me," said Gar, not sure right now if he wanted to slap Josefina or kiss her. All he knew was that he needed to keep a close eye on her because he had a strong feeling that she was going to do something stupid. And next time, she might not be so lucky as to just walk away from everyone and everything. Especially him.

Josefina opened the door to the hull and climbed down the stairs, not really needing to check the cargo, but wanting an excuse to get away from Gar. It didn't seem that he remembered what happened last night. For that, she was ever grateful. No one seemed to know she'd lain in bed with Gar while he was naked and she was barely clothed. Since no good could come from telling the truth, she wanted to keep it a secret.

She walked down the steps, stopping and sitting at the

bottom of the wooden staircase. The hull was filled with crates and barrels, but bilge water covered the bottom of the floor. Thankfully, the crew had put the cargo up on raised platforms so the goods she had to sell at the trade fair wouldn't be ruined.

Suddenly, fear crept in and she started doubting that she could really run her late husband's business by herself. If her brother-by-marriage were here, things would be different. Josefina knew all about the inventory and pricing, but Clovis was the one who kept things, as well as the crew, in line. Everyone liked him and listened to him. She, being a woman, had a tough challenge ahead of her. Especially with the crew, men who all seemed to despise taking orders from a woman. The main one being Lord Gar.

She heard a noise at the far end of the hull, and looked up, squinting her eyes trying to see in the dark since she hadn't thought to bring a lantern. It had sounded like wood scraping over wood.

"Hello? Is someone down here?" she called out, standing back up, peering through the darkened area. As the ship rocked back and forth, the bilge water splashed upon the raised platforms and even the sides of the crates. She didn't want to step in the water, so stayed on the stairs. "Show yourself," she called out, slowly standing, wondering who was hiding amongst the cargo.

"There she is," came Cup's voice from the door at the top of the stairs.

"Josefina, what in heaven's name are you doing down there?" asked Martine, peering into the darkened hold. "It is nasty down there and it stinks. There are probably rats running around, so be careful," she continued to call out warnings. "You're going to ruin your gown with the bilge water."

"I wanted to check the cargo," she called back, looking once more to the far end of the hold but not seeing anyone. She started wondering if it was just a rat she'd heard, like Martine had mentioned. Josefina truly hoped she wouldn't encounter any rats.

"Let the crew do that. Come back to the deck anon," Martine told her. "It's not safe down there."

"Mayhap you're right." Josefina headed up the steps, looking over her shoulder once more. That's when she swore she saw a shadow that looked like an outline of a person from the corner of her eye. Or had she? It was there and then it was gone. It all happened so fast that mayhap she'd only imagined it.

"We're going to be in Scarborough soon," Cup told the women, helping Josefina back to the deck and closing the door to the hold. "Cap'n wants me to escort both of you back to the cabin until the ship is docked."

"Lord Gar needs to stop giving me commands," said Josefina, trying to deal with this ongoing situation.

"I think it might be best," said Martine, putting her hand on Josefina's arm. "Besides, I have something I want to talk to you about in private."

"Oh, I see. All right," agreed Josefina, worried that Martine knew her secret, after all. Either way, it would be nice to have someone to confide in. Martine was the only other woman on the ship and there was no way Josefina would ever confess to a man that she was attracted to rude, arrogant, Lord Gar.

Once they were in the cabin, Martine closed the door

behind them. Josefina had thought Robin was in here sleeping, but she didn't see him so figured he left to help prepare the ship for docking.

"The trade fair should be a good one." Josefina sat down on the bed on this side of the curtain. "It will be quite busy."

"I'm sure it will." Martine sat on the bed next to her. "Now, tell me what happened with my cousin last night."

"What?" Josefina sprang to her feet and started pacing. "I don't know what you mean." She wrung her hands in worry.

"I think you do." Martine stood as well. "When I went to sleep you were in this bed," she said, pointing to the bed with the crumpled sheet and messy blanket where Josefina had lain with Gar. "And when I awoke, my cousin was in the bed instead. Naked. And you were nowhere to be found."

"I left the cabin," said Josefina, about ready to burst, wanting to tell someone about it. Still, she was being cautious. She didn't really know Martine and wasn't sure she should open up with her feelings to her. Especially since she was a noble and Gar was her cousin.

"You left?" Martine raised a brow. "I am sure you didn't go onto the deck at night. Not alone and with that crew! And by the looks of the condition my cousin was in, I'd say he had been sleeping here most of the night. So, that means you were here with him." She was just too clever for her own good. Josefina wasn't going to be able to hide the truth from her any longer.

"Oh, all right, he was here with me." Josefina's heart beat furiously. "I was in bed when Lord Gar came into the cabin last night, drunk. He— he disrobed and laid down next to me, trapping me here with his arm and leg holding me down."

"He what?" Martine looked to be shocked as well as amused. She giggled.

"It isn't funny," snapped Josefina. "I was trapped beneath him and couldn't leave if I wanted to."

"Well? Did you?"

"I told you I left, but it wasn't until I could move his body off of me this morning."

"That's not what I'm asking." Martine's eyes flashed to the door and then she lowered her voice. "Did you make love with him?"

"What? How can you even ask such a ludicrous thing?"

"You were in your shift, and he was naked and drunk," Martine pointed out. "Besides, I know my cousin when he gets around women."

That caused her concern. "Are you saying he kisses women he barely knows all the time?"

"He kissed you?" Once again, Martine's eyes opened wide.

"He did, but that was earlier." Her fingers touched her lips, memories filling her head of how he tasted. "He said it was just to teach me a lesson."

"A lesson? What kind of lesson?"

"Oh, Martine, it doesn't matter. I was furious at him, but at the same time I find myself oddly attracted to him. Is there something wrong with me?"

"Nay, of course not. It is normal to have feelings for a man."

"But I'm a widow. I should be in mourning over Donald."

"You already told me why you don't mourn him. But did you love him at all?" asked Martine, reaching out and taking Josefina's hand.

"Nay. I can honestly say there was no love between us. And only lust on his end. In the short year we were married, we only coupled a handful of times."

"Oh. I see. Well, then I'd say there is nothing wrong with you at all. You are just starved for the attention and affection of a man. Even if it is someone like Gar."

"I am?" asked Josefina, making a face. "So, are you starved for affection too? I mean, since you are not married?"

"I admit, I would like affection from a man, but being a noble I will most likely have to marry someone of my status, just like Gar has to do."

Josefina's head snapped up in surprise. "Gar has to marry someone of his status?" she asked, not liking this idea for some reason.

"Aye, of course. He's a noble. Besides, it is the king's order. As soon as this trip is over Gar will not be able to sail again until he finds a noblewoman to wed, settles down and has an heir."

"I see," she said, letting out a deep breath. "I suppose that is the life of a noble."

"Yes, for the most part."

"So, anything at all that might have happened or may happen in the future between us means nothing after all."

"Never say never," Martine answered with a shrug of her shoulders. "After all, my brother as well as several of my cousins married commoners."

"They did?"

"Our Uncle Corbett is not happy about it since he is trying to bring back honor to the family name, but the fact remains that it happened."

There was a quick knock on the door and Gar stuck his head inside. "Has anyone seen Robin?" he asked.

"Nay," Martine answered.

"Have we docked?" asked Josefina. "I'm in a hurry to get my tables set up at the trade fair."

"Yes, we've docked," said Gar.

"I better tell the crew where to bring the cargo." Josefina hurried out the door.

"Where the hell is Robin?" growled Gar. "He's supposed to be keeping an eye on you two."

"I'll go with Josefina. We'll be fine together. Calm down, Gar." Martine hurried after the other woman.

Gar was about to leave the cabin when he heard a noise that sounded like a loud yawn. It came from behind the hanging blanket. Gar walked over and pulled the blanket aside to find Robin sitting up on the hidden bed, stretching.

"What the hell are you doing?"

"I was sleeping, since you left me on watch most of the night, or did you forget?"

"You are supposed to be watching over the women."

"Oh, don't worry, I have been."

"With your eyes closed?" Gar crossed his arms over his chest.

Robin yawned and stood up. "My eyes might have been closed, but I assure you my ears were wide open."

"What does that mean?"

"It means, I know that Josefina has feelings for you, Gar."

75

"She what?" This took Gar by surprise. He slowly unfolded his arms and dropped them to his sides.

"I also know you slept naked in bed with her last night trapping her under your arm and leg. And she was only wearing her shift."

"So, I wasn't dreaming after all." Gar ran a hand over his hair. "She fancies me, does she?" He cocked a half-grin.

"That is what it sounded like to me." Robin strapped on his weapon belt and yawned again. "Of course, I was half-asleep and mayhap I heard wrong."

"Cap'n, come quickly," shouted Cup from the door to the cabin.

"What's wrong?" asked Gar.

"When the crew started unloading the cargo, they found something they didn't expect."

"Now what is going on?" Gar hurried to the main deck with Robin right behind him.

"Throw him overboard," said Solobow as Gar walked up to find everyone crowded around in a huddle.

"Keel haul, keel haul," chanted a few of the crew members.

"What's going on here? Move aside and let me through." When Gar got to the front of the crowd, he saw Two Spit holding a young, lanky and very dirty boy by one arm. He wore a tattered tunic and trews that looked to be too short with holes in them. There were no shoes on his feet.

"We found this stowaway in the hold," said Two Spit. "What do you want me to do with him, Cap'n?"

"I say we string him up from the yardarm," said Hothead Harry, anger in his eyes.

"Nay, leave the poor boy alone." Josefina pulled the stowaway over by her and Martine.

"We don't need another mouth to feed," complained Whiney Wilkens. "I say we bring him to shore and leave him there."

"I'll handle this," Gar called out. "Crew, lower the gang-plank and unload the cargo. Now!"

"Aye, Cap'n," the men answered going about their work.

"Give me the boy," said Gar, reaching for the stowaway. "I'll teach him a lesson."

"Nay!" Josefina stepped in front of the lad with her arms out. "You can't hurt this stowaway, and neither will I let you send anyone away."

"Josefina, don't start this with me again. Stowaways will not be tolerated."

"This one will," she said, looking back at the lad who was talking with Martine. She took a step closer to Gar and for a second he thought she was going to touch him, but she didn't. She put her face up to his, but it was only to speak softly so the others couldn't hear. "Don't you see?" she asked.

"See what?"

"This isn't your normal stowaway at all."

"He looks like an average beggar and thief to me," said Gar, looking over her shoulder at the lad with short hair and dirt all over his face. He was very young, but Gar wasn't sure of his age. Still, he looked to be not more than a child.

"Lord Gar, sometimes you can be so blind that I am surprised you are a sea captain at all."

"If you have something to say, then do so, Josefina. I have things to do."

"This stowaway will stay on the ship and be under my protection from now on."

"Your protection? That is absurd."

She looked back at the lad. "Your men and even you are fooled easily, but I am not, no matter what you think."

"I beg to differ," he mumbled.

"Lord Gar, this stowaway is not a young lad at all. This stowaway is a girl in disguise."

"Holy hell," said Gar, biting the inside of his cheek so hard that he tasted the tangy flavor of blood. His life was going from bad to worse quickly. How in heaven's name was he expected to do his job when he would now have three females on board?

CHAPTER 6

Josefina's heart went out to the stowaway. Even though she was in disguise and dressed as a boy with her hair cut shorter than either a boy or girl would wear, there was no doubt in her mind. This was a girl. "What is your name?" she asked the girl who seemed to be very young.

"Please don't punish me. Don't hurt me," begged the child. "I am an orphan and have nowhere to go. I haven't had food to eat for days now. Only some apples I found in a barrel in the hold."

"Josefina, you need to instruct the crew where to bring the cargo," interrupted Gar. "Tell them where to set up for the trade fair."

"I will. Just a moment." Josefina took the girl by the hands. "I am Josefina. You are safe with us. Now, tell me your name and how old you are."

"My name is Etta," said the girl. "I am . . . thirteen years old. My parents are dead and I have no siblings. I am all alone." The poor child looked thin and gaunt and very small for her age. She might even be sickly.

"You need to get cleaned up. And we will get you some food to eat."

"Josefina, would you rather I handle everything for the trade fair?" asked Gar becoming extremely impatient.

"Nay. Nay, I'll do it," she said, wanting to go instruct the crew but at the same time not wanting to leave Etta. The girl seemed so frightened. Josefina's heart went out to her. She wanted to know why the orphan was on the ship, but decided she'd ask her later. Right now, all that mattered was her well-being.

"I can tend to Etta and get her washed up so you can instruct the men," offered Martine.

"Oh, thank you," said Josefina. "Etta, this is Lady Martine. You can trust her."

"My lady." Etta half-bowed, half-curtseyed, not seeming to know exactly what to do.

"Lady Martine will help you get cleaned up and find you something to eat. I have to go ashore now, but she will bring you to my stalls at the trade fair later." Josefina looked up and nodded at Martine who nodded back in agreement.

"Thank you, Lady Martine and Lady Josefina." The girl attempted to curtsey again, losing her balance and stumbling forward. Gar reached out and grabbed her to keep her from falling.

"Josefina is not a lady," Gar told Etta. "But I am Lord Gar and the captain of this ship," he explained to her in a gruff voice. "Do you know what happens to stowaways?"

"Please, don't hurt me, Lord Gar." The girl dropped

down to her knees. "I'm sorry, but I had nowhere else to go and was frightened."

"Lord Gar! You are scaring her," said Josefina narrowing her eyes in frustration. While she was trying to calm the poor child, Gar was coming across as a beast. She hurried forward and helped the girl to stand. "Go now," she told Etta, directing her to Martine who put her arm around the girl's shoulders and took her back to the cabin.

"What do you think you're doing?" asked Gar. "Stow-aways won't be tolerated. They never are."

"She is only a child."

"One who needs to learn her place."

"And what do you suggest we do with the poor, fright-ened girl? Have her walk the plank and feed her to the sharks?" snapped Josefina. "Is that the type of punishment you see fitting?"

Gar found himself tongue-tied when he heard Josefina's sharp words. There was no doubt she was referring to him as a pirate again. If not, she would never have said *walk the plank*. He didn't like that. He wanted Josefina to see him in a different light, but he wasn't sure she ever would.

"Of course, I don't want that," he said softly. "But you need to think how this will look to the crew if we let a stow-away stay on board without even being punished."

"Are you afraid of what the crew is going to think of Etta?" she asked. "Or what the crew might think of you instead?"

"What kind of a thing is that to say?"

"You need to hear it from someone, Gar."

"Lord Gar," he corrected her.

"Lord Gar," she said with a roll of her eyes. "Be yourself,

no matter who that might be. Do what feels right in your heart. Don't do something only because it is what has always been done in the past."

"You don't understand."

"Don't I?"

"It is what's expected of a sea captain, not to mention, a noble. So, you're telling me to just break the rules?" he asked.

"I don't know," she responded with a shrug. "Remember, I am not a noble and don't have the same silly rules as those with a title. However, yes, that is what I'd do."

"It's not that easy, Josefina. One of a higher status has to do as is expected. Yes, I'm sorry to tell you that nobles do have rules that we need to live by. Even if I don't always agree with them, or like them."

"Well, mayhap it is time you change the things in your life that you don't like instead of living by rules that will harm an innocent young girl." With that, Josefina left Gar standing there, hurrying over to instruct her crew unloading the boxes and barrels from the hold.

"What was that all about?" asked Robin, coming to Gar's side.

"I'm not sure," Gar answered, his eyes fixated on Josefina. She was naught but a commoner, but a feisty one at that. This woman was so different from anyone he'd ever met before. As absurd as she sounded telling him to break rules and do what was in his heart, she made a good point he supposed. This woman was not afraid to challenge authority. That wasn't always a good thing, but Gar liked her ferocious nature.

Josefina was determined and headstrong and not afraid

to voice her opinions. She actually held a lot of qualities more commonly found in a man. He chuckled. Actually, he liked spunk in a woman and would love to find such spirit in a noblewoman who was like Josefina. Gar enjoyed a challenge and she certainly gave him one. He never thought he'd tolerate a woman acting this way, but something about her made him start to question his beliefs.

Josefina seemed to have no fear of anyone or anything. She also held the words of wisdom of a sage. That somehow touched Gar's heart. What the hell was happening here? The girl went against everything Gar ever believed in, and for some reason... for some reason, it all made damned good sense to him right now.

"Did you want me to escort Josefina to land, to set up for the trade fair?" asked Robin.

"Nay," he answered, shaking his head. "I'll do that. You wait for Martine and the stowaway. Bring them to shore when they are ready."

"What are you going to do about the girl they found hiding in the hold?" asked Robin.

"Nothing," said Gar, still staring at Josefina. Damn, this woman had such strength about her and with that came a sense of unspoken power. With no husband and all alone, she still forged forward with every intention of running the family business by herself. Not many women he knew would be so bold or so daring to even consider such a thing.

"Nothing?" asked Robin, shaking his head in disbelief. "Did you say you're not going to do anything at all about the stowaway?"

"You heard me."

"Well, even if you're not going to punish her, you

certainly can't let her stay on the ship. It's not right. Besides, it's highly ridiculous. There are too many girls on board already. Plus, I don't need another one to watch over and protect. You're going to leave her on shore, right?"

"I haven't come up with definite plans yet," said Gar, finally turning to look at Robin. "But whatever I decide, it'll be for the benefit of the orphan, I assure you."

"What are you saying?" Robin perused him as if he were mad.

"She's a girl and all alone, for crissakes! What kind of a man would I be not to see to her safety? Of course, I'll do whatever it takes to make sure she is taken care of in every way."

"Somehow, I get the feeling you're not talking about the stowaway anymore, but instead you are speaking of Josefina," said Robin, looking at him curiously. "Am I right?"

Gar shrugged and flashed a smile, turning and hurrying after Josefina, not wanting to let her out of his sight.

He watched as the crew hauled the cargo up to the main deck from the hold of the ship. Rolling the barrels and dragging the crates they moved to the gangway of the ship. Being a flat bottom ship, they could dock in shallower waters. This slowed the ship down, but made it better for carrying cargo as well as keeping it steady at sea. Several docksmen secured a wagon at the foot of the plank leading from the ship. The crew slid or rolled the cargo down to them and they loaded it onto the wagon, preparing to take it to the village green. That is where the stalls were set up for the fair.

"Careful with those crates!" shouted Josefina, running over to Hothead Harry as he picked up a wooden crate and tossed it to Two Spit Sam. "There are eggs in there. It is fragile and I don't want the eggs broken."

"Mmmph," grunted Harry, tossing another crate to Two Spit, not paying heed to her warning.

"That's enough!" Gar stepped in to intervene. "You heard Josefina. If any of those eggs are broken, you two will have it taken out of your pay."

"We're sorry. We'll be more careful," said Two Spit, holding the crate under his arm and purposely tip-toeing to the gangway, causing the rest of the crew to burst out laughing.

"Thank you," Josefina told Gar. "I'm finding it challenging getting these men to listen to me."

"You didn't really think it would be easy, did you?"

"I suppose not." Her head snapped around and she raised her arm in the air. "Solobow, careful with that. Those boxes are filled with fine silks and expensive cloth. It cannot get wet."

"Aye, I hear ya," said the man, continuing to work.

"This ship has journeyed to many foreign lands, hasn't it?" asked Gar in admiration. He'd never sailed that far before, usually staying in the channel or the North Sea, but would love to take the *Lady Josefina* into uncharted waters and to different lands since Gar loved to explore.

"My husband was always traveling and never home," Josefina told him, keeping her eyes on the crew and the cargo. "I honestly don't know all the lands he's sailed to, but I can tell you he did a lot of trade. We have exotic spices and fine silks all the way from the Orient."

Gar whistled long and low. "That is one hell of an agenda."

"Yes. And also one that never included me," she said under her breath.

"I thought you didn't like to travel aboard a ship, so why does it even matter that you didn't go with him?"

She looked at him from the corner of her eye. "It would have been nice to at least be asked."

"I see." Gar understood now why the widow didn't seem to be in mourning. It was starting to sound as if their marriage was mostly in name only and that she and her late husband never spent much time together. He thought about it for a minute. He supposed if he were married to a woman who didn't like to sail, he would leave her behind rather than to give up his love of the water too.

"I know what you're thinking," she said, looking the other way and wrapping her arms around herself.

"Do you, now?"

"You think my husband had relations with other women in every port."

He chuckled. "I didn't even consider that, but now that you mentioned it, did he?"

She turned to look at him without saying a word. Her eyes were glassy and her lips were pressed together in a firm line. The joy and life he'd seen in her gaze was quickly replaced with sadness and despair.

"Forget that I even asked that," he mumbled, feeling awkward now. "You don't need to answer, Josefina."

"Nay, I want to answer," she said, her sadness seeming to be replaced by anger now. "Donald always had whatever he wanted. That is part of why he was so successful being a trade merchant. He always had money, but never spent it on me."

"It's really none of my concern." He looked down and straightened his tunic, feeling really uncomfortable with this conversation. Now, he regretted bringing it up at all.

"Yes," she continued, on a rampage now. "That included him paying whores for sex at every port. He never admitted it to me directly, but I have eyes and ears. I know what goes on behind my back."

"Well, mayhap you're wrong. Perhaps he was just one of those men who engulfed himself in his work and that's all. Mayhap it had naught to do with other women."

"Oh, it did, I assure you. The physician told me that Donald died because of a disease. A disease he contracted from coupling with too many unclean women. Those were the doctor's exact words."

"Oh, I'm sorry." That surprised Gar. He never thought she'd admit that to anyone, and especially not him. "I really hope you didn't—" He stopped midsentence, realizing he was sounding rude.

"I didn't," she said, biting her bottom lip. "Donald and I only made love a few times during the two years we were married. I assure you, once I heard these rumors, I didn't let him touch me at all."

"Good, good," said Gar, not feeling comfortable with this conversation and wanting to take Josefina's mind off of these nasty things.

"Good?" she gasped.

"Nay, not good. I mean, not good that it happened and he became ill. I was talking about you. Good that you didn't let him touch you so you weren't infected as well."

She glared at him and he realized he was only digging a bigger hole to fall in. He needed to change the focus quickly.

"So, the docks look crowded today and the crowd will only grow larger as the day goes on. The trade fair should be very busy."

"That is what I'm counting on," she replied, brushing away a stray tear with the back of her hand. "I want to sell everything Donald brought back from his overseas trips because I don't want anything to remind me of— of what happened. I want it all gone."

"All gone?" That surprised him. "Josefina, you have a hundred and fifty tuns in the hold. That is one hell of a lot of merchandise to move. You can't expect to sell it all."

"Then I will trade it for more practical things that even commoners would want or be able to buy."

"There will be a lot of other vendors here at the fair who will be competing with you."

"I will do whatever it takes. I won't stop until it is done."

"But it is too much. Will the wares even all fit in one stall?" he asked her, knowing they wouldn't. Not unless some sort of magic was done.

"Nay. I wanted to get here early because I need to pay for three stalls. And they will all be filled to the brim with my wares."

"Three stalls?" he asked in surprise. "That will add up immensely in cost."

"I know. I will pay two shillings for each stall to the burgesses. I am quite prepared to do so." She shook the pouch of coins at her side to prove her point.

"How will you take care of all the customers with three stalls of goods to watch over? That is absurd. You cannot do it yourself."

"Clovis and his wife were supposed to be here to help

me. However, when my brother-by-marriage broke his leg, his wife announced she was staying home to care for him. I'm on my own now but I will find a way."

"You shouldn't have to handle this alone."

"All right, that is enough on that cart," she called out, stretching her neck to see how much had been loaded on to it. "Take it to the village greens immediately. Bring another one up as fast as you can. We have no time to waste. Quickly. Go!" she instructed the men. The small wagon creaked as they rolled it away, packed to the top with crates stacked so high they were threatening to topple over.

"You'll need help at the stalls," Gar pointed out, following her down the plank to the pier. "If nothing else, you'll need someone to watch to make sure nothing is stolen while you handle the money."

She stopped at the bottom of the plank and turned around. "Are you offering to help me, Lord Gar?" she asked with a raised brow.

"Well, I— I —" Gar didn't know how to answer. He hadn't meant that. After all, he was a noble, not a merchant. His place was sitting in the tavern drinking whisky or walking the streets conversing with other nobles. He was also a captain and needed to keep an eye on the ship. It was beneath his status to do the work of a merchant and he just couldn't help her.

"I didn't think so." She turned and walked away at a brisk pace.

"Wait, Josefina," he called out, hurrying after her, dodging the dockworkers and merchants with every step. A good dozen ships were already anchored in the harbor. The crowded dock was a sign that it was only going to get busier as they approached the area where the trade fair would be held. "You can't do this alone."

"I won't be alone," she told him over her shoulder, following her cart of wares. "I'll have the crew to help me."

"The crew?" That almost made him shudder. Only one or two of the crewmen would actually follow her orders. And Gar didn't think any of them were trustworthy enough to collect and handle money for the goods sold. "Are you sure that is a good idea?"

She stopped again and spun around to face him. "I don't know what you want me to say. Nay. Nay, of course, it isn't a good idea, is it?" she asked, waving her hands in the air. "After all, men like Hothead Harry or Two Spit Sam will not only scare away potential customers, but probably bring ruin to my business in one way or another."

"Then don't have them help you."

"I have to. I need to. I don't really have another choice, do I?"

"Perhaps you should have thought of this before coming on the journey. I'm sure you must have known some trustworthy people in your village who would have been willing to help you sell and trade your goods."

"Nay. Nay, I didn't." Her face became bright red. "You see, no one wants to help a widow who has taken control of her late husband's business. Even though it is allowed through the guild, it is still not accepted by many. No one believes I can carry on my husband's business because after all, I am just a woman."

"I'm sure no one really thinks that," lied Gar, since it was his thought exactly. "I mean that you can't handle the business, not that you're a woman. That part is obvious."

"I don't really care what they or you or anyone thinks." She turned and started away. "Now, please leave me alone. I have a lot of work to do and not much time to get it done. I need to stay focused."

"Josefina," he said under his breath, stopping in his tracks and watching her go. His head told him not to do it, but his heart told him otherwise. The internal struggle was strong and he didn't like this. All he wanted was to sail the ship of his dreams, but this was turning into a nightmare quickly. "Damn it," he spat, turning and looking back at the ship. How the hell was he supposed to know what to do? Did he dare risk his reputation and go against the rules a noble lived by? Then again, he was already going against the rules by letting that stowaway get away unpunished. And by having not one but two women on board.

He looked back at Josefina once more, then shook away the cobwebs in his head. Turning on his heel he made his way back to the ship where he belonged. Back to the only *Josefina* who wouldn't give him more problems.

CHAPTER 7

"Cup, put these flutes on the table," said Josefina, handing the cabin boy a box of wooden handmade flutes that her husband had gotten somewhere along the way. "And, Two Spit, you are in charge of the weapons," she instructed.

"Aye, I like that," chuckled Two Spit, pulling a sword out of a crate and holding it up to admire it in the light. It had a wooden handle carved with snakes.

"I want to manage the weapons." Hothead Harry dropped a crate he'd been carrying and raced over and yanked the sword away from Sam.

"Hey, give that back." Sam reached over the table, but Harry held it up and away from him.

"Stop it, you two. We don't have time for your pettiness. Now, I need help unloading the silks and fine linens in the next stall. Who will help me?"

All the crewmembers who were working with the boxes stayed silent and looked the other way. She realized that the last thing rough men like these wanted was to be seen carrying bolts of cloth.

"Never mind, Cup will help me."

"What?" Cup had his head in a box and emerged with flutes in each hand. "I thought you said I'm in charge of the instruments. I don't want to handle cloth."

"Fine, I'll do it myself," she said with a sigh, realizing Cup and the men had dirty hands anyway. They would probably soil the material if they as much as touched it. She would never be able to sell soiled silk and lace. "Wilkens," she called out. "Have you put those eggs in baskets yet?"

"I'm workin' on it, but a lot of them are broken," he answered.

"Nay. I knew that would happen." With her hands on her hips she scowled at Harry and Sam who had been tossing the crates of eggs around. She was ready to wring their necks. She would have scolded them if she hadn't been so afraid they'd walk away and leave her stranded there by herself.

"Just put out the good ones but keep the broken ones on the side. You can cook them up for the crew later."

"Aye," said Whiney Wilkens. "But the men don't like shells in their food."

"Josefina, there is more cargo in the hold," said T-Bald, putting a box down on the table and scanning the area. "However, I don't think you'll be able to fit any more items in just three stalls. What did you want me to do with it?"

"You're right," she said, feeling a knot in her stomach. "Bring whatever perishable goods are left, but leave the rest on the ship for now. We'll bring the boxes out one at a time as needed after I make some sales. Or mayhap I'll use the rest at the trade fair when we get to Scotland."

"Aye. I'll tell the captain," said T-Bald, leaving and heading for the ship.

Thankfully, it was nice out and the weather was fair this autumn day. But the crowds were growing quickly. Vendors carrying trays with loaves of freshly baked breads and pies walked back and forth, calling out, already selling their goods.

"Buy my bread. White for the nobles, and brown bread for everyone else," said a man resting a large tray of bread on his shoulder. As he walked past, the delicious aroma wafted over to her on the breeze, making her hungry.

"Hand pies for a penny," called out another vendor even louder. Small pies the size of one's hand and made from berries and nuts were stacked on his tray. A little boy tugged on his mother's skirt and they stopped to buy one.

A fishmonger walked by with a cart filled with fish, the scent assaulting Josefina's senses. She hoped he wouldn't be setting up anywhere near her fine silks.

A strolling minstrel approached next, stopping at one of her stalls. She heard the beautiful sound of flute music as she unfolded her silks, thinking it was the minstrel playing. But she stopped when she heard the minstrel playing his gittern. He strummed the pear-shaped guitar with its rounded back and gut strings, playing along with the flute music. Looking over to the instruments, she noticed Lady Martine and Robin standing there with the stowaway, Etta. Etta's face was clean and her hair combed. She wore an oversized tunic belted at the waist to look like a dress. And on her feet were a pair of soft, slipper-type shoes.

"Etta?" Josefina put down the bolt of cloth and hurried over to the table with the instruments. "You play the flute?"

"I told her not to touch it," said Cup, sounding as if he thought he would be in trouble. "Put it down." Cup reached for the flute but Josefina's hand shot out to stop him.

"Nay. Let her play. It is beautiful music. Etta, you will stay here with me in the stall."

"You're going to let a stowaway help you sell your wares? Is that smart?" asked Robin in a warning voice.

Etta slowly lowered the flute. "I don't know how to count money," she told Josefina.

"And neither do you need to. I just want you behind the table playing the flute. It'll bring customers over."

The minstrel nodded and smiled, walking away playing his gittern.

"You want me to stand behind the table with you and play the flute?" The girl seemed shocked, surprised and a little frightened at the same time.

"I cleaned her up and lent her a pair of shoes," said Martine. "She was too small to fit in my gowns, but we made one out of one of Gar's tunics." Martine smiled proudly.

"Gar's tunic?" asked Josefina, wondering how angry Lord Gar would be when he found out his cousin gave a stowaway the clothes of a noble. It made her laugh inwardly.

"Yes, because my brother wouldn't give up one of his." Martine glanced at Robin.

"I'm going to the inn to secure rooms for us for the night before they are all taken," reported Robin. "Martine, are you coming with me?"

"I don't know. I'd rather stay here and help Josefina since it looks like she needs help."

"Oh, would you?" asked Josefina, suddenly feeling relieved. "I would love another woman here to help oversee the sales of the fine silks for the nobles, and the bolts of cloth."

"Martine, you are a noble," Robin reminded her. "You shouldn't be doing the work of a commoner."

"I wouldn't mind," Martine answered, ignoring her brother and stepping behind the table, laying out the silk, lace and bolts of cloth. "Oh, you have some fine materials here, and I know all about them. I will be able to sell to the nobles easily for you."

"I have jewelry as well that only the nobles would be able to afford," Josefina told her.

"Let me watch over the higher-end items," said Martine. "I even know about spices." She nodded at the spices on the table.

"Thank you!" Josefina was so happy that she hugged Martine. "Etta, keep playing the flute and draw people over."

"All right, said the young girl, doing as instructed.

"How am I supposed to secure rooms for us and watch over you two at the same time?" asked Robin.

"We're fine, Robin. Now go." Martine swished him away with her hand. "You are standing in front of the stall and no one will be able to see the wares."

"I don't know if Gar is going to like this."

"We are perfectly safe," Josefina told him, working as she spoke. "We are at a trade fair and behind the tables. No one is going to bother us. Besides, I've got some of the crewmembers here with us." She nodded to the men. Harry and Sam were still squabbling over the weapons while Solobow decided to juggle eggs in the air.

"Solobow, put those down before you— "

Too late. He dropped one and it broke on his foot. A stray pig in the streets waddled over to lick it up while children ran by chasing a barking dog.

"This is going to be a long day," she mumbled under her breath.

"Hothead," said Crusty Rusty, approaching the stall. "Cap'n is looking for you back at the ship. He wants you to watch over things so he can go to the tavern for a drink."

"Me?" Harry let go of the sword. Two Spit grinned, having won. He held it with two hands now.

"You are his first mate," Josefina reminded him. "Go! Rusty can stay in your place."

"Let me see that sword," said Rusty, ducking under the table and coming up next to Sam. Once again, the squabbling began. God's eyes, she hoped to sell all her wares quickly because she didn't know how much of these men she could take.

CHAPTER 8

Gar downed a swig of ale, sitting at a small table with Robin in the Screeching Owl Tavern and Inn. On the ground floor of the establishment was a tavern, with rooms upstairs for rent. The tavern was crowded and the noise level high.

"Did you get rooms for us?" asked Gar, leaning forward to be heard.

"They only had one room left," replied Robin. "But it has four beds in it, so it'll do nicely."

"I don't know," said Gar, thinking about Josefina. "You know the ladies won't want us in the same room."

"God's eyes, Gar, so what? Martine is my sister and your cousin. What difference does it make?"

"Josefina will be there too," Gar reminded him, burying his nose in his tankard, trying to drown his thoughts and desires for the beautiful woman.

"What did you say? Talk louder." Robin leaned forward, trying to hear over the noise.

"Josefina," he said.

"What about the ship?"

"Not the ship, the girl."

"Oh, you want to be alone with her in the room. I understand. We can arrange that. No problem."

"Nay! I never said that."

"Huh? You don't want to bed her then?" Robin scrunched up his face. "Really, Gar, sometimes I worry about you. I mean, the girl is pretty and awfully available. No one would think badly of you if you were to couple with her."

"Must I remind you, I'm supposed to be looking for a noblewoman to marry," said Gar, motioning for the server to fill up his tankard once more. A young boy filled his cup and also Robin's before leaving the table.

"Aye, that's right. You need a noblewoman." Robin raised his tankard, looking over the top. "There's one. How about her?" he asked, gazing across the room.

Gar turned to look, almost falling off his seat. She was a noblewoman all right, but also looked as if she could win an arm-wrestling match against Hothead Harry.

"Nay," he said, cradling the tankard in two hands. "I don't think so."

"Then how about her? Or mayhap that one?" asked Robin, nodding to two noblewomen over by the drink board. They weren't ugly, but not nearly as attractive as Josefina.

"They're probably married, so that won't work."

"Married? How can you tell?" Robin cocked his head and squinted, eyeing up the women.

"There are two men with them."

"They could just be escorts."

"If so, the women wouldn't be in a tavern. Nay, they're married. Just forget it."

"You know, I think you only have eyes for one girl and don't even want to consider others. But must I remind you that one girl is not a noble?"

His gaze shot upward. "I have no idea who you mean."

"I think you know exactly who I'm talking about." Robin chuckled. "Cousin, I see the way you come to life when you merely look at Josefina. And you've already been to bed with her— naked. So why deny your needs and wants?"

"I have no interest in Josefina or anything she says or does. And I already told you we didn't do anything together," said Gar under his breath. His gaze shot back and forth, hoping no one was listening to this absurd conversation.

"Martine says Josefina fancies you too," continued Robin.

"What?" Gar's heart skipped a beat when he heard that. "Really?" His gaze dropped back down to his tankard again. "Josefina likes me? What did she say about me?"

"I thought you weren't interested in her. Mayhap you are after all?" A silly grin crossed his face.

Gar couldn't deny his feelings for Josefina. But neither did he need to admit them aloud. Nothing good could come of it. He knew what was expected of him and he just needed to push these thoughts away. He shook his head. "Nay! I told you, I'm not interested." He downed the ale in three swallows and banged the empty tankard down on the table. "I have my orders from the king. I am to find a noble-woman to marry or I'll never sail again. So, that is just what I'll do." He stood up abruptly, pulling a coin from his pouch and plunking it down on the table. "Give that to the innkeeper and ask him to have a hot bath set up in the room tonight."

"A hot bath?" Robin looked befuddled.

"For the ladies, not me."

"You say ladies, but you know Martine is the only lady among us."

"You know what I mean. Now finish up and get back to the stalls at the fair and watch over the women. That's your job, so do it."

"Where are you going?" asked Robin, finishing off his ale, belching, and collecting the coin Gar threw down.

"I'm going back to the ship."

"I thought you had Harry watching over it for you."

"Aye. But it's like asking the wolf to watch over the lambs. I don't want to leave him alone too long."

"You don't trust him?"

"Not in the least."

"Then why did you leave him on the ship to begin with?" Robin pushed up from the table.

"I don't want him to know I don't trust him. If so, it'll only prompt him to do something I know I won't like."

"You make no sense, Gar."

"I'll meet up with you later tonight. I have some things to take care of first."

Gar left the tavern, making his way through the crowded streets, heading back to the docks. He couldn't stop thinking about Josefina and how she was bravely taking on more than she could handle. Guilt ate away at him. Mayhap he should have helped her after all at the trade fair. He couldn't trust the seedy crew. Besides, Martine was doing so, and she was a noble. Then again, Martine was sailing on a ship filled

RIDING OUT THE STORM

with lusty men and she shouldn't be doing that either. It was in Martine's nature and the nature of every woman in his family to be rebellious and outrageous.

"Crap," he said, turning around and taking a shortcut down Butcher's Row. He made his way to the village green where the vendors had set up stalls and were selling and trading their wares. He decided he just couldn't leave Josefina in such a bond. She didn't deserve that. The woman needed help. He decided he would be the one to help her, after all.

"Please. Give me a ha'penny, my lord," said a beggar man in tattered clothes following after him with his palm outstretched. Gar wasn't against giving the poor money, but not in such a crowded place like this. If he did, before he knew it, he'd have a swarm of beggars around him pulling at his clothes. Nay, bringing out coins and tossing them to the crowd now wasn't a good idea in the least.

He stopped and looked over his shoulder. "I won't give you coin, but I'll give you food."

"My lord?" the man asked in confusion, looking hungry and hopeful.

"Follow me," he said, leading the way to Josefina's stalls. Unfortunately, by the time he got there, he had a line of about twelve beggars trailing behind him. He felt like the damned Pied Piper.

He stopped, seeing Josefina taking money from a noble. "Thank you," said Josefina, putting the coins in the pouch at her side. Then she took a swag of silk from Martine and handed it to the noblewoman. Looking up, her eyes met with Gar's. She stopped, watching as he came closer. "What are you doing here?" she asked.

Before he could tell her he was there to help her, the beggar behind him spoke up.

"The lord is going to feed us all for free."

"Aye, we need food," called out a beggar woman from behind the man, holding her two young children close to her ragged skirt.

"He's going to do . . . what?" Josefina looked at Gar and blinked several times in succession.

"I told the man I'd give him something to eat," Gar tried to explain.

"And what about the dozen people with him?" Her arms crossed over her bosom and she scowled.

"I only promised him, but I guess more followed me here."

"Yes, I guess so." Josefina didn't look or sound happy at all about this situation. "And what, Lord Gar, were you planning to do? Deplete me of all my fruits and vegetables? I am here to make money you realize. I need something to live on now that I no longer have a husband."

"Nay, that's not it at all. I swear, I wasn't planning on giving away your food and profits."

"Then how exactly are you planning on feeding all these people?" asked Josefina, waiting for an answer. She didn't like the fact that Gar was promising to give away what wasn't his to give.

"We're hungry," called out the little boy. "Please, we need some food."

"My children haven't eaten in days," said the woman with him. "Please, don't let us starve."

"Oh, Josefina, we have to help them," whispered Martine from behind her hand.

"I know, but I can't be giving away my product to beggars," protested Josefina. "If so, I'll be throwing away my profits."

"You can't give away your food? Really?" Gar raised his eyebrows and nodded. When she turned to see what he was looking at, she sighed. Etta was eating an apple, because Josefina had told her to help herself to the food.

"That is different," said Josefina.

"Is it, now? Beggars, orphans, they seem the same to me. Plus, I see the girl is wearing what looks like my tunic if I'm not mistaken. So, are you giving away my things now without even asking?"

"Don't be angry with Josefina. That was me who gave your tunic to Etta," Martine explained. "But Gar, she needed clothes. Hers were ragged dirty and falling apart."

"Just like these people?" he asked, holding out his arm to encompass the beggars who had followed him here.

He kept staring at Josefina and it made her nervous. Nobles started passing up her stalls when they saw the group of dirty beggars hovering around her tables. Those with status wanted to be nowhere near these dirty, stinky vagrants. No one even came up to the tables again since Gar had brought the beggars here. Word would pass to others in the fair and she'd be lucky to have any more nobles as customers for the rest of the day.

"Josefina, what are you going to do?" asked Martine.

"Besides kill your cousin?" she asked softly, looking down and straightening out the lace on the table. When she looked back up, all the beggars were staring at her with wide, pleading eyes. They looked so pathetic, helpless, and dirty. Their clothes were bedraggled and most of them stank. She wasn't sure they'd ever had a bath in their lives. "Fine," she said, letting out another sigh. "Go ahead, Lord Gar." She held out her arm, pointing to the tables that held the eggs, nuts, spices, dried fruits and root vegetables as well as apples.

Gar walked around to the back of the tables, sensing that Josefina really hated him right now. He had only meant to help her, but things took a wicked turn and not in his favor. Now, if he fed the beggars from her table, he'd be more or less stealing from her. That wasn't what he wanted at all. He wished now that he had thought things through before he told the beggar to follow him. With the way things were going, next, Josefina would be calling him a pirate again. And he supposed that this time, she wouldn't quite be wrong. He spied the broken eggs in a basket. There were dozens of them next to Whiney Wilkens. The man had a small iron brazier and a fire going in it. Atop the grates he had a pan heating on the fire.

"What are you doing?" he asked.

"Me?" asked Wilkens. "I'm going to cook up some fish heads for me and the boys, since we're hungry." He nodded at Rusty, Sam and Cup.

"That will have to wait." Gar picked up a large wooden bowl and handed it to him. "Start scooping out these broken eggs, and make sure to pick out all the shells."

"Whatever for?" asked the man.

"Because you are going to cook up some eggs for these poor people." He nodded at the beggars.

"Naw, why should I? They are just beggars. They can't have our food." He pulled the basket of broken eggs closer.

"Our food?" asked Josefina, hearing what he said and

coming over to join them. "Don't you mean my food, Wilkens?"

"Aye. That's what I meant," muttered the cook, tending to the fire.

"Lord Gar, I don't mind feeding these beggars. But only these twelve, no more," she said looking directly at Gar. "If so, I will be losing too much in profits."

"The eggs are already broken and not saleable anyway," Gar pointed out, wondering how much she would really be losing in profits by giving away ruined food.

"Fresh bread and butter. Buy my bread," called out a merchant, passing by with a tray of round loaves of brown bread and lugging along a wooden pail of freshly churned butter.

"Over here," Gar called out, holding his hand in the air. "How much?" he asked the vendor.

"My lord," said the vendor with a big smile, trying to bow while holding the tray filled with bread. He eyed up Gar and thought for a moment before answering. "Four pence, my lord. And that includes some butter."

"What?" growled Gar. "I can buy nearly a dozen eggs for the same price. I know you are hiking up the price just because I'm a noble."

The man became flustered, being caught trying to get more than twice what the bread was worth from him just because Gar had money.

"I meant, that is for the entire tray of bread," the vendor corrected himself, trying to save his hide. "It's two pence a loaf, my lord. With butter."

"Of course, it is," said Gar, knowing exactly the game the man played. "Give me the bread."

The man reached up and took one loaf off his tray and handed it to Gar.

"Nay. I want the entire tray of bread and also that pail of butter," Gar explained. "I'll give you two shillings for all of it." He held out the money.

The seller's eyes opened wide in surprise and excitement.

"Are you sure, my lord?" asked the man, knowing he was being paid much more than the worth of his goods.

"Ask again, and I'll take it back."

"Nay, my lord. Thank you, my lord. Thank you."

Gar paid the man while Cup took the tray of bread from him. Etta retrieved the pail of butter.

"Lord Gar? What are you doing?" asked Josefina, eyeing up the large tray, having overheard what he paid. "You paid much more than the worth of what you got."

"I know that, Josefina. I just wanted to teach the man a lesson. If he's honest, he'll win in the end."

"You with the lessons again," she said with a sigh.

The aroma of fresh bread caused the beggars to push even closer to the table.

"I will feed the twelve of you only," Gar said to the beggars. "But once you have your food, you must roam the streets eating it, and tell everyone that this stall is selling it. You will not tell anyone you got it for free. Do you agree?"

"Aye," said the old man, speaking for all of them. "We will do whatever you wish if you'll just give us a bit of bread, my lord."

"I'll do better than that. I will give each of you scrambled eggs atop a hunk of fresh bread slathered with butter."

The beggars grew excited at the thought of eating so much good food.

"Start cooking," Gar told Wilkens. "Use the broken eggs only. And I don't want to hear any complaining," he warned the man before he could whine about it. He looked at Josefina next. "I'll pay for the broken eggs so you won't lose any profits." His reached for his money pouch.

"Nay," she said, holding up her hand to stop him. "I don't want your money."

"Fine," he said, lowering his hand. "Then, take it out of my pay at the end of our trip."

"No, I won't do that either," she told him. "I pay to feed the crew and was going to use the broken eggs for them. Plus, because of Lady Martine's help, those last noblewomen who were here paid me a very good price for the silk."

"So, what are you saying?"

"I'm saying that I appreciate what you're doing, but it is not needed."

"I think it is."

"You are doing a good thing, not only feeding the beggars but marketing my food which will bring me more sales." She reached into her pouch and pulled out the amount he'd spent, handing it to him. "I will pay."

Josefina watched Gar's gaze drop to her hand but he did not take what she offered. He looked highly insulted.

"Don't," was all he said.

"Then, I'll add this to what I'll pay you at the end of our journey."

"Nay, Josefina. I am the one who wanted to feed the beggars, so I'll pay."

"But you are helping me to make profits as well."

"And that is exactly what I wanted to do." He looked into her eyes. "You asked me earlier for my help and I denied you. I want to make up for that now."

"Oh, that is kind of you." She slowly replaced the coins in her pouch.

"You see, I am not really the ogre of a man you think me to be, Josefina."

She saw a kind, caring side to him that made everything else he did to upset her up until now seem trivial. Because of it, she wanted to show him that she had a good side to her, too. "Here. Add this to the eggs," said Josefina, causing Gar to turn around. She held up a bundle of leeks. "And this," she said, picking up some dried parsley and handing it to him.

"Oh, I bet these people have never tasted herbs and spices before," said Martine, picking up a jar of dried saffron and inspecting it.

"The saffron is too expensive. It will bring in a good price from the nobles, so we can't use that," said Josefina. "But I would be willing to share some rosemary and sage." She handed the two jars to Gar.

"Are you sure about this?" asked Gar, taking the spices from her.

"Yes," she said, raising her chin and staring deeply into his eyes. "You paid for the bread and butter and the least I can do is give these poor people some broken eggs and a few spices. I am sure it will mean the world to them."

Gar took his knife from his waist belt and grabbed a loaf of bread. "Cup, help me slice this bread. We have some meals to make and I am going to help."

Josefina had been reluctant at first to give away free food, but Gar had turned her loss with the broken eggs into a major profit by the end of the day. Those twelve beggars had taken their food and went out in the crowded marketplace just as Gar had instructed. They told everyone where to get the tasty eggs with leeks and spices served on fresh bread with butter.

Her stalls were three times as crowded as they were earlier. She ended up selling most of her produce. The nobles stopped by again, buying swords, jewelry, silk and lace and even more. The saffron brought in a good amount of money, just like she knew it would. And because Etta played the flute so beautifully, it attracted musicians, children, and of course the parents of those children too. Everyone wanted wooden flutes, causing her to run out by the end of the day.

The crowds were diminishing as the night air blew in. The last rays of sun disappeared on the horizon as the merchants all covered their stalls, settling in to sleep next to them to keep thieves from stealing their wares during the night.

She spread blankets over the wares on the table, with Cup helping her. Martine and Etta left with Robin hours ago, heading to the rented room at the inn.

"Allow me," said Gar, taking a blanket from her, covering the rest of the weapons.

"Thank you, Lord Gar," she said shyly.

"I decided I don't care about what others think of me after all. Just like you said."

"I see that and I appreciate your help. Your idea to have those beggars show off the food really brought in a lot more sales than I'd expected." She shook the heavy-laden pouch of coins at her side.

He looked down. "Is that all the money you made today?"

"Nay, there are two more pouches just as full. I had Rusty bring them back to the ship earlier. I told him to leave the money pouches in your cabin."

"Aye. They'll be safe there."

"My entire body aches. I am tired and hungry," she said.

"I'll take you to the inn. I had Robin tell the innkeeper to have a hot bath waiting for you and Martine. I'm sure by now Martine is finished."

"A hot bath?" Her voice cracked. "That sounds wonderful."

"I've sent for Solobow and T-Bald to sleep out here by the stalls tonight to guard your wares."

"I think that is a good idea," she answered, trusting those two more than the rest of the crew. "Where will you sleep?" she asked.

"There is... we only have one room," he told her.

"Oh, that's right," she answered. Her cheeks blushed and she quickly looked away.

"I will take you to the inn, but I'll be spending the night on the ship," he informed her.

"You will?" Her head snapped upward. Why did it bother her that he wouldn't be in the same room as her? Mayhap because she felt safe with him? Or was it just because she wanted to feel his arm thrown over her as she slept again?

"I have to guard the ship and the cargo in the hold," he told her. "And the money pouches."

"Of course. As you should," she said, her tongue darting out to lick her dry lips. "I suppose we should go then."

"Yes. Hold on to my arm," he told her. "It is dark and the streets have deep ruts. I don't want you to fall."

"As you wish, my lord." Josefina held on to Gar's arm as they made their way through the darkened streets and toward the inn. When they passed by a tavern on Grope Street, several whores in the doorway called out to Gar.

"Are you in need of release, my lord?" asked a dark-haired woman with her bodice tied so tightly that most of her large breasts were popping out the top.

"I can show you a good time," said a red-head, hiking up her skirt to expose her bare leg. She raised it so high that Josefina saw her bare woman's mound beneath the skirt as well.

"Oh!" cried Josefina, gripping tighter to Gar's arm. "I don't like it here."

"And neither do I, but this is the way to the inn."

"Let's turn around," she said. "We'll go to the docks instead."

"Josefina? What are you saying?"

"I don't want to go to the inn and right now I don't care about a bath either. I just want to get away from all these people. Let me go back to the ship with you. Please."

"You are saying you want to sleep on the ship?"

"Lord Gar, I just want to... I want to be with you."

"So, you don't think I'm a pirate anymore?"

"You proved today that you do have redeeming quali-ties," she teased, smiling.

"You'll be safe on the ship. And you'll be on your side of the hanging wall blanket," he told her. "Let's go back to the ship. It is the place I like to be."

"Me too," she said with a yawn, holding on to his arm as they walked to the docks. Honestly, she didn't care about ships at all and didn't even like being on the water. However, she knew Gar loved these things. And if he was going to be there, then, right now, that was also where she wanted to be.

CHAPTER 9

As much as Gar was tempted to kiss Josefina again, or perhaps do even more, he didn't. The last thing he wanted to do was to push himself on the woman. He admired her tenacious ways and respected her for not only carrying on her late husband's business, but also because she fed the beggars, knowing it was what he wanted to do.

Aye, it was in the contract that she was in charge on this trip. As much as he hated that, he didn't want to make her life any harder. She'd already lost an unfaithful husband and was now left to carry out his work on her own. Josefina wasn't so bad after all, he thought to himself. He laid on his bed on one side of the blanket wall, knowing she was so close, right on the other side. She deserved someone better than that scurvy dog of a husband who treated her like dirt. Gar wanted to give her things that she'd never had before. Mostly, he wanted her to feel loved. And he wanted to be the one to make her feel special.

He flipped over on the mattress feeling hot and bothered

ELIZABETH ROSE

just thinking of her. She was so close right now, but at the same time so far away. Untouchable. That is what she was to him. Off limits. He couldn't risk falling in love with a woman who wasn't noble. Nay, there was too damned much at stake for him right now.

Besides, Josefina deserved someone better than him. Even if he made love to her, it would only hurt her in the end. Nothing could ever come of it. He'd been ordered by the king to wed a noblewoman, marry and settle down, and have an heir. It was his only way out of this tough situation. Life on the water and sailing ships was his passion. Was he really ready to give up his dreams just for one night with Josefina? If he coupled with her, he knew it wouldn't be just a one-night thing. He'd want her even more, and he couldn't allow that.

He rolled over on the bed again, feeling ever so restless. Mayhap he could just... kiss her. Nay, he'd never be able to stop there. The girl looked like an angel with her long, flowing hair. He couldn't stop thinking of her pouty mouth with those full lips that were just begging to be kissed. And her eyes. Her beautiful windows of her soul were her most enchanting asset. Acorn-colored with a tint of ochre swirls, they were bright and intense in a very alluring way.

He tossed and turned some more. And when he rolled back the other way, he got the distinct feeling someone was watching him. With his hand under his pillow, he gripped his dagger and shot up to a sitting position, holding out his blade.

"Stay back!" he shouted.

"Oh! Nay!" shouted Josefina, jumping backward. She'd been standing next to his bed in just her shift. Her hair was

RIDING OUT THE STORM

long and loose and mussed. Her eyes looked hooded and sleepy. "Gar, it's me," she cried, not using his title. It was intimate and he liked that. It made him feel closer to her somehow.

"What's the matter?" He jumped out of bed, forgetting he was wearing nothing but his braies. "What's wrong? Has someone entered the room to steal the money?" He held out the blade in one direction and then the other, scoping the room for intruders.

"Nothing is wrong and no one is trying to steal a thing. Now, please put down the blade." She gently placed her hand on his arm and he lowered his weapon. Her eyes lowered as well. "Please, put on your trews, if you don't mind."

Suddenly, he felt like a scoundrel. "Of course," he said, making his way in the dark to the back of the chair where he'd left his trews. "Why are you up? Do you need something?" He stepped into his trews as he spoke.

"Nay. I just couldn't sleep and heard you tossing and turning as well. I wanted to ask you if we could go for a walk up on deck."

"I don't know," he answered, pulling his tunic over his head. "Most of the crew is still on the ship, remember. It's not safe to be out there in your nightclothes. You don't know what might happen."

"I suppose you're right," she said. "I'm sorry to disturb you. I'll go back to bed." She turned to leave, but he wasn't ready to let her go.

"However, if you donned your gown and cloak and stayed close to me, we could go up to the sterncastle and look at the stars," he suggested. "The men aren't allowed up there while the ship is docked so they won't bother us."

"Oh, I'd like that," she replied. "I was hoping the fresh air will help me to relax so I can fall sleep."

She quickly dressed while he lit a lantern. He had her long blue cloak waiting when she appeared on his side of the blanket wall again. He held the cloak out for her, meaning to help her don it.

"Thank you," she said as he placed the cloak around her shoulders and lifted her hair out from underneath. Gar breathed in her scent. She smelled like sweet herbs or flowers. Her hair felt like spun silk in his hands and he caressed it with his fingertips, wanting to always remember how soft it was.

"My pleasure, my lady," he said, not even realizing what he'd said until she turned back to look at him in surprise with those big round eyes drawing him in.

"You called me a lady," she whispered. He swore he saw her bottom lip tremble in the light of the lantern.

"Aye, I guess I did." He couldn't help himself from reaching out to cup her cheek in his palm. "You are so beautiful that I guess I forgot for a moment that you are not a noble." He let his thumb glide across her bottom lip, feeling the slight moisture, wanting to taste it more than anything right now.

"Are you going to kiss me again to teach me a lesson?" she asked, almost sounding as if that were an invite and that she wanted him to do it.

"I'm sorry about that kiss," he told her, honestly meaning it.

"So, does that mean yes or no?" Her voice was gentle, the

harsh edge of her earlier tone today now completely gone. She seemed so sweet and soft-spoken. He was drawn to her like a moth to a flame.

"I— I promised you I wouldn't do that if you came back here to sleep. I am a man of my word." He started to release her, but her hand shot out and clamped on to him.

His heart jumped and his eyes interlocked with hers.

"I know," she told him. "I can see now that you are a gentleman and not a cur after all." To his surprise, she stood on her tiptoes and brushed her lips against his in a kiss, causing him to want to forget all about his promise. His body reacted and his libido made it hard for him not to throw her down on the bed and rip off her clothes, burying himself to the hilt between her curvy hips until she cried out in passion.

"I think we'd better go out into the cool night air before I make a liar out of myself." He grabbed the lantern and turned and opened the door.

She followed, stopping in the doorway and looking back at him. "I almost wish you would," she said, staring up at him with hooded eyes.

Confusion set in, and he wasn't sure what to do. He took her by the arm and quietly led her over the deck, stepping around the snoring crewmembers sprawled on the floor, sleeping in every nook and cranny on the deck.

"Shhhh," he said with his finger to his lips, silently guiding her up to the sterncastle, and leading her to the railing at the back of the ship. The autumn breeze was gentle tonight. There were barely any clouds in the sky at all. The stars shone brightly above them while the full moon illuminated the deck. "Here is the best place to stand to look at the stars." He guided her to the railing.

"Oh, it is beautiful up here," said Josefina, gazing up at the sky. "There are so many stars. I don't think I've ever seen this many in one place before."

He chuckled.

"What's so funny?" she asked.

"This is nothing compared to a moonless night at sea. You'd swear each star in the sky was naught but a grain of sand on a beach somewhere up high."

"I've never heard that comparison before," she answered in amusement.

"Just look at it out there. See where the moon shines down on the water, making it look like a streak of light, guiding the way right back to us?" He seemed so excited, pointing it out over the water. Gar's eyes lit up in excitement and his entire face came to life.

"You really love sailing on the ocean, don't you?" she asked him, wanting to know more about him.

"I do," he admitted, leaning with both elbows on the wooden railing now.

"Why do you love it so much?" she asked.

"Why? Just look at it out there, Josefina. What is there not to love? It's so peaceful and beautiful. Sailing and being on the water has always taken away my worries and made me feel so free."

"I guess that is one way to look at it." She shivered in the breeze and he noticed.

"You're cold."

"Aye. Aren't you?" she asked. "You are not even wearing a cloak."

"Nay, the cold doesn't bother me," he told her. "Here, let me keep you warm." He stood behind her, cradling her in his embrace. "Better?"

"Mmmm. Much better." She looked back at him and their faces were so close now that they almost touched. She saw his gaze fasten on her mouth and she was sure he was going to kiss her. She wanted him to return the kiss she'd boldly given him in the cabin. Sadly, he refrained from doing so. "Tell me about yourself," she said. "I'd like to hear about your childhood."

With her back pressed up against his chest she felt the rapid rise of his heartbeat when she said this.

"You want to know about my time living with pirates," he said.

"I've heard rumors that your own mother was once a pirate. Is that true?"

"She was," he said softly, his arms still around her. "But it was only because as a baby she and her twin brother were stolen by pirates."

"Stolen? Oh, that is horrible."

"My mother, Lady Echo, grew up thinking she was the daughter of the infamous pirate, Captain Powell ap Llyr. She lived on the *Seahawk*, but left me on shore being raised by whores."

"What?" That surprised her. "Why would she do such a thing?"

"It was to protect me from the crew, the weather, attacks, and just everything," he told her.

"Who was your father? Where was he during this time?"

"My father, Edgar Blackmore, was brothers with the father I have now, who is really my uncle."

"The Lord Warden of the Cinque Ports," she said with a nod. "So, what happened to your father?"

"He's dead."

"How did it happen?"

"I'd rather not talk about him anymore if you don't mind. Instead, I want to know more about you."

"You already know about my late husband, Donald," she told him. "And you know that my father is Bartholomew Woods, the shipwright who built the *Lady Josefina*."

"Aye. But what about your mother?"

"She is alive and well. She's at home with my father. They are both very old."

"Do you have siblings?"

"I have two brothers who are also shipwrights, but they are nearly twenty years older than me."

"So, you were raised mainly as an only child."

"Yes, I guess you could say that."

"So was I, really. Although I have three half-sisters."

"Yes, Lady Martine told me."

"Josefina, look at me," he said, turning her around.

She stared up into his eyes, feeling as if he wanted to say something important.

"What is it, Gar? I mean, Lord Gar," she quickly corrected herself. "I am sorry, I keep forgetting to use your title."

He put a finger to her lips and smiled slightly. "I like it when you forget, but don't let anyone know that." Then, she was pleased when he leaned over and kissed her, just like she'd been wishing he would do all night. "I hope you don't think I'm a liar now that I kissed you after I said that I wouldn't."

"I don't mind," she admitted. "I kind of hoped you would. What were you going to say?" she asked him. "It sounded pretty important."

He stared at her intently for a moment as if he were thinking. Then he shook his head as if trying to brush away a thought. "It's not important. But what is important is that we both get some sleep. If the trade fair tomorrow is anything as successful as today, we're going to need all the energy we can get."

"I know you're right," she said, leaning forward, giving him a big hug.

"What is that for?" His deep voice vibrated against her chest since they were pressed so closely together.

"I suppose it is because I've decided I really like you, after all," she told him.

"And I, you," he said, kissing her atop the head.

"Thank you for being yourself, Gar. I like seeing the real you and not just the man you think you need to be for everyone else."

He didn't respond to that. It almost seemed as if what she said upset him and she didn't understand why.

"Let's get back to the cabin," he told her. And just like that, the intimacy between them was gone.

CHAPTER 10

"He kissed me last night," Josefina told Martine the next morning as they laid out the remaining silk and cloth on the table at the trade fair. It was early yet, but already the vendors were all setting up their stalls. The sky was overcast today and it looked and smelled like rain.

"Who kissed you?" asked Martine, folding up a square of blue silk.

"Gar. I mean, Lord Gar."

"What?" Martine's head popped up. "I'm sorry my cousin is being so rude. I'll have a talk with him and tell him to stop that at once."

"Nay. You don't understand," said Josefina. "I rather liked it."

"You did?" Martine made a face. "I don't know how anyone could enjoy kissing Gar." She faked a shudder to show her disapproval.

"Neither of us could sleep last night."

ELIZABETH ROSE

"Now I know why you two didn't come to the inn. By the rood, Josefina, please don't tell me he bedded you?"

"Calm down. Nothing else happened." Josefina laid her hand on Martine's arm. "However, part of me almost wished it would have."

"What on earth are you saying? You can't actually mean that."

"I am saying that your cousin isn't at all the crude, demeaning man I first thought he was. He proved that yesterday when he helped out at the trade fair. Not to mention, it was his thoughtful, caring idea to feed the beggars, which ended up bringing in more sales for me in the end. He has a kind-hearted side to him after all."

"Don't let one kind action fool you. As long as I've known Gar, he only thinks about himself. So, if he did something nice, it was only because there was something in it for him."

"I don't know why you speak so badly about your cousin. I really wish you wouldn't."

"It's happening. Again." Martine shook her head.

"What is?" asked Josefina with a smile.

"My family all seem to be falling in love and marrying commoners lately. We are nobles and are supposed to marry someone of our own status! Especially Gar. You are just infatuated with him, but it will pass in time."

"Did you say love? And marriage? I never said anything about that." Just hearing Martine's words made Josefina's heart beat faster. For a mere second she pictured herself married to Gar, but her common sense made her push the thought from her head. Mayhap she was only infatuated after all. She'd recently lost her husband. She was feeling so overwhelmed, as well as alone. Could that be why she was so drawn to Gar? Did she need or want another man in her life to take care of her? She was confused and no longer sure.

Martine continued. "It sure seems as if the two of you are smitten with each other. I didn't expect that since you both seemed to hate each other just a few days ago."

"Yes, I suppose that is true." Josefina had never changed her mind about someone this fast, but Gar was different. He was hurting from his past just as much as she. It almost seemed as if being together helped ease pain for both of them. "Martine, I was wrong. I thought that way about him only because I knew nothing about him. I do now. I think I've seen a side of Gar that he hides from others. He is really a thoughtful and kind man under that gruff exterior."

"Hah!" Martine laughed. "I wish I could believe that, but I won't fall for it."

Josefina's smile faded. "What does that mean?"

"Everyone knows the last thing my cousin wants is any kind of commitment with a woman. Don't get me wrong, he likes women. A lot. However, he is not the marrying type. Please don't get your hopes up concerning Gar, Josefina. If you do, you are going to be let down and hurt."

Josefina felt confused by this. Gar didn't seem that way at all lately. It upset her to hear Martine talk about him this way. "You say he'll never marry and settle down, but I thought he was ordered by the king to get married, so he will do so after all."

"Aye. Let me rephrase that. He will get married, but to a noble and only because he has to. And even though he'll fight it to the death, he will do it in the end because it is what's expected of him. He cares much about what others think about him."

"Are you sure about all this?" asked Josefina, all her hopes of possibly something more growing between she and Gar fading fast.

"Gar loves sailing and the sea. He lives for it. It is his passion."

"Yes, I know that. He told me," she answered.

"He will marry a noblewoman because he doesn't want to lose his privilege of sailing ships like the *Lady Josefina*," Martine explained. "He will do whatever it takes to get what he wants. And what he wants is to be able to continue sailing. Mark my words, it is true."

The wind picked up and Josefina shivered, pulling her cloak closer around her. Then she felt a few raindrops and noticed the sky getting darker.

"We'd better pack up the silk and fine linens. They'll get ruined in the rain," said Josefina. Even though the stall was under a canopy, the rain blew in all directions and would get all her products wet.

"Josefina, it's starting to rain harder," called out Crusty Rusty from over by the weapons. "Shall I pack up the swords so they don't rust?"

"Aye, I suppose we'll have to," she said with a sigh, looking up at the sky. It didn't seem like the rain would let up any time soon.

"What about the food?" asked Whiney Wilkens from the far end of the stall.

"Whatever bread is left, wrap it up," she told him. "Only leave out the root vegetables, eggs, and apples. Only the things that won't be ruined by the rain."

"Aye, I will," said Wilkens. "Although, it would do us all good to get in out of the rain," he complained in his usual manner.

"Cup, have Etta help you spread out the product we have left," instructed Josefina. "Hopefully, there will still be customers today and the rain won't scare them all away."

"I would but I don't know where Etta is," said Cup. "I haven't seen her at all this morning."

"Really?" She turned to Martine. "Didn't Etta come back from the inn with you this morning?" she asked.

"Nay, she was never there," said Martine. "She said she wanted to wait for you when we left for the inn. Robin and I thought she was with you and Gar."

"Nay, she wasn't." Josefina quickly scanned the area but didn't see Etta anywhere. "I'm going to go look for her. I'm worried about her."

"Nay," said Martine. "Robin and Gar will be back soon. I'll send them out to look for her when they return."

"I can't wait that long. It is about to start pouring, and I don't want the poor girl to get sick. She doesn't even have a cloak." Without waiting to hear Martine object again, Josefina pulled her cloak tighter around her and stepped out from behind the stall.

"You can't go alone," protested Martine. "You should have a male escort."

"Well, I don't have one."

"At least take Rusty or Wilkens with you."

"I'm not going anywhere," said Wilkens, overhearing them. "If I don't put away some of this food, it won't even be fit for the crew to eat."

"And I've got to watch over the weapons and be here to take coin from any sales," protested Rusty.

"I'll go with you, Josefina," offered Cup, even though he was a young boy and couldn't do much to protect her if trouble should occur.

"Thank you, Cup. We need to move quickly. The sky is about to open up. I don't even know where to look for her."

"Yesterday, I heard her talking to some of the whores from the Red Lantern Tavern. They were trying to get Etta to come with them, so mayhap she is there."

"God's eyes, I hope not!" said Josefina, realizing he was talking about the tavern with the whores on Grope Street. It was the same one she'd tried so hard to avoid last night. The last place she wanted to go was back there, but she didn't have a choice. Etta was only a child and Josefina had to protect her. "Hurry, Cup. We might already be too late." Josefina took off at a run with Cup right behind her.

As they approached the Red Lantern, Josefina started wishing she had waited for Gar and Robin to return after all. The whores who solicited Gar last night were standing in the doorway. Josefina felt very nervous, but figured she'd just ask if the women saw Etta and get her answer and leave.

"Excuse me, but have either of you seen Etta? She is the young girl who helped me at my stalls yesterday." Josefina barely breathed as she waited for her answer.

"You mean the girl playing the flute?" asked the buxom redhead.

"Yes. Have you seen her?"

The women laughed.

"What is so funny?" asked Josefina.

"She's not leaving here. Not when she plays such fine music. The men like it and from now on she'll be playing the flute while we pleasure our customers," said the dark-haired whore.

"She's doing what?" snapped Josefina, shocked to hear this.

"We've all had a very prosperous night because of her. The men love to hear music as we couple with them. It gives them rhythm is what they said."

"Oh, nay!" Josefina covered her mouth, horrified by the thought. The rain started to come down faster. "Send her out here, right now. She is only a child and doesn't belong in this type of establishment."

"We're paying her a ha'penny and a meal a day, so don't think we're treating her poorly," said the redhead. The whore sounded as if she thought there were nothing wrong with this and that they were doing Etta a great favor.

"Cup, go in and find her and bring her out here right away," instructed Josefina, not wanting to enter the tavern herself.

"All right." Cup took a step forward, but the women stopped him by blocking his path.

"If you want her, go in and get her yourself," the dark-haired wench told Josefina in challenge. "After all, we saw how you charmed that English lord last night. He would have paid us well for our services, but you pulled him away from us and we're not happy about it."

"Nay. That's not true. I didn't do anything like that. It was Gar's idea to leave," said Josefina in a shaky voice, feeling trouble brewing.

"Gar?" The redhead raised her brows. "Did you hear that?" she asked her friend. "She doesn't even use his title."

"She bedded him!" said the whore's friend. "Don't let her leave until she pays us the money that he paid her."

The women both grabbed Josefina, pulling her to the door of the tavern.

"I'm not a whore! He didn't pay me anything. You've got this all wrong," shouted Josefina, struggling in their grips.

"Let's bring her to Rock," said the redhead. "He'll get the money out of her one way or another."

"Nay, leave her alone!" Cup tried to fight them, but the whores were too tough. One of them actually punched Cup in the eye and knocked him down.

"Cup! Get out of here," Josefina called out to the boy before he was hurt worse.

"I won't leave you," Cup called back. One of the whores stomped down hard on his foot and Cup cried out, hopping on one leg, holding his foot.

"Please. Go and get Gar!" Josefina begged Cup as the whores pushed her into the tavern, blocking the door so she had no chance of escape.

Josefina stumbled and fell to the ground. The floor was covered with spittle and wet, smelly rushes. Quickly, she got to her feet, brushing off her hands.

"Josefina!" came a voice from the stairs leading up to the whores' rooms.

Josefina looked up to see Etta being hauled down the stairs by a burly man. Etta had a flute in her hand and was dressed in scanty garments. They'd combed out her hair, frizzing it, and putting ribbons in it as well. Her face was painted heavily, just like a whore's.

"Etta! Are you all right? Did they hurt you?" Josefina ran to the girl, pulling her out of the man's hold. Etta hugged Josefina, crying.

"Ebony? Scarlett? What the hell is going on here?" growled the man from the tavern, calling the whores by name.

"Rock!" called out the two whores, strolling across the tavern, wiggling their hips as they walked, never stopping trying to attract another client.

"This girl stole a good customer from us last night," said the redhead named Scarlett.

"He was a noble and would have paid good coin for one or even more for both of us." The dark-haired tart that was called Ebony pulled her bodice lower to expose more cleavage.

"No one takes business from my girls and gets away with it," said Rock in an angry voice. "Hand over the money the lord paid you. Give it to me now."

"I wasn't paid anything by Lord Gar, and we didn't do what you think we did." Josefina, clung to Etta's trembling body.

"I'm waiting, and I'm not a patient man. Now, hand over all your money." Rock held out his open palm. When she did nothing, his gaze dropped to the coin pouch attached to her belt.

"Josefina, give him the money pouch," begged Etta. "If you don't, he'll hurt us."

As frightened of this man as Josefina was, she didn't want him or the whores to know it. Once she showed her fear, things would only get worse. She needed to stay strong. Not only for herself, but also for poor Etta.

"Nay!" she spat, dropping her hand to cover her coin pouch. "This money was made from selling silk and food and weapons at my stalls. I am a trade merchant, not a whore." She looked at the girls when she said it. "I will not give you a single penny because this is my money."

"I would give Rock the coin pouch if I were you," warned Ebony.

"Aye," agreed Scarlett, biting at a hangnail. "Rock's punches will land you on your ass, and something surely will be broken."

"Nay!" cried Etta, her wide eyes filled with fear. "Please, give them what they want, Josefina. Then we can leave here."

"Who said anything about leaving?" asked Rock, looking them both up and down. "I think you two will make a nice addition to my team."

"What?" asked Scarlett in a shrill voice. "Nay, we don't want them here."

"We work this tavern alone and won't share our clients with them," screamed Ebony.

All hell broke loose next. The girls came for Josefina and Etta, and Rock stepped in front of them, grabbing each whore by the neck.

"I don't like this this kind of behavior," Rock warned the whores. "I'm going to take it out of your pay for causing trouble."

That's when Ebony bit his hand and Scarlett tried to hit him. Rock punched Ebony in the face and pushed Scarlett to the floor. Etta cried out in fear.

"You two, come with me." Rock's hands gripped around

their wrists so tightly that Josefina thought he would break their bones.

"Nay!" shouted Josefina, struggling against him as he started to climb the stairs. "Let us go."

"You heard the lady," came a voice from the doorway. Gar stepped in, drawing his sword. The patrons scattered, not wanting to be in his way.

"I got Lords Gar and Robin, just like you said," Cup called out to Josefina.

"Oh, you're the lord who bedded this whore, taking money away from my girls," said Rock, referring to Josefina as a whore.

Robin was right behind Gar and unsheathed his sword as well.

"She's not a whore!" Gar rushed across the room, his sword held high, meaning to bring it down on Rock. Rock pushed Josefina and Etta down the last two stairs, pulling a dagger from his boot and lunging at Gar. They hit the floor, punching each other, rolling around in the dirty rushes.

"Kill him, Lord Gar!" shouted Cup.

"Nay," screamed Scarlett, helping Ebony to her feet. "Knights aren't supposed to walk in and kill us off. That's not noble."

"He's a pirate! He'll gut you all," said Cup, sounding excited by the idea.

Several of the patrons inched forward, but Robin held them off with his sword pointed outward. "Stay back," he warned them.

Gar had the upper hand, getting atop Rock on the floor, putting his blade to the man's neck.

"Go ahead, pirate. Kill me, you scurvy cutthroat," snarled Rock.

"I will, just because of that comment," said Gar, his anger taking control.

"Gar, nay! Please don't kill anyone," begged Josefina. "You are better than that. Don't let them taunt you into doing something I know you'll regret. You don't really want to kill him."

"Of course, he wants to kill me," said Rock. "Just look at him. He truly is a pirate."

Gar wanted nothing more than to slit the cur's neck, not only for calling him a pirate but for Josefina and Etta's sake. But Josefina's sweet voice begging him not to hurt the man, made him hesitate.

"Did he or anyone hurt either of you?" he asked Josefina.

"Nay. I'm not hurt," answered Josefina. "Etta, did they do anything to you?"

"Nay," said the girl, tears streaming down her cheeks. "They just made me play music. Josefina, I want to leave here."

"Me too," said Josefina. "Gar, please let him go and take us back to the ship."

It was against his better judgment to just walk away in this situation, but he didn't really want to kill anyone and definitely didn't want the girls to see him do it. He picked up the man's dagger and threw it across the floor. Then he slowly moved his blade from the man's throat. "I warn you, touch either of my girls again, and I will slit your bloody throat next time without a second thought." He got up, still holding the sword in his grip. "Robin, get the girls and let's get the hell out of here." He held out his sword, walking backward to the door after Robin, Cup and the girls. It wasn't until they left the tavern that he turned around and sheathed his sword.

"Thank you," said Josefina.

"Why the hell didn't you wait for us before coming here?" asked Gar.

"Cup told us what happened and we came right away," said Robin. "You girls shouldn't be out in the town without an escort."

"It's done and over with, so let's not speak of it again." Josefina put her arm around Etta as they all made their way back to the ship in the pouring rain.

"I should have used this," said Etta, pulling out a dagger and showing it to Josefina.

"Where did you get that?" she asked.

"I stole it from one of the whores," said Etta.

"Put that away before you hurt yourself," growled Gar. "Robin, go get Martine and tell Rusty and Wilkens to pack up the goods. We set sail tonight."

"Pack up? Set sail?" Josefina's head popped up. "But the trade fair just started. I'm not leaving yet. The fair will probably last for a month."

"You are under my protection, and I will not let you stay here another day," said Gar. "I know men like Rock. He won't just let this go. He'll be back to get you and Etta, mark my words."

"That's why you and Lord Robin are here. To protect us," said Josefina.

Gar looked up at the sky. "This rain isn't going to break anytime soon. It'll probably rain solid for at least the next week. Did you really want to sit here that long, hoping it clears up?"

"I want to leave here, like Lord Gar said," Etta told Josefina, still crying. "Please. I don't want that mean man to come looking for us. I don't want to go back to the tavern. Please, Josefina. Can't we go?"

Gar noticed Josefina glance up at him and then back to the girl. They continued walking to the ship while Cup and Robin went back to the stalls. Josefina stopped for a moment to remove her cloak and put it around Etta's shoulders since the girl was shivering from the rain.

"I suppose I made enough yesterday that it won't matter if we leave early," said Josefina in a soft voice. "Perhaps we can stop back on our return trip. I can also try to sell the rest of the goods at the Dunbar trade fair once we get to Scotland."

"Thank you," said Etta. Once more, Josefina looked over at Gar.

Gar thought she'd be furious that he suggested they leave the trade fair. Instead, in her eyes, he swore he saw gratitude. The rain drenched them. Josefina's wet hair clung to the front of her bodice. He wanted more than anything to reach out and push a wet strand of hair from her face, but he didn't. He was falling too fast for Josefina and needed to keep his distance from her. If not, he'd be disobeying a direct order from the king, not to mention putting all he cared about at risk. Nay, he couldn't have feelings for Josefina because she was naught but a commoner.

He felt her cold hand reach out and touch him on the arm. "Thank you, Gar," whispered Josefina, her teeth starting to chatter from the cold as she smiled. She reached up, meaning to kiss him on the cheek but Gar pulled away.

Damn, all he wanted to do was to kiss her and hold her right now, but he couldn't. He shouldn't. He'd been so unsettled seeing her in the tavern with Rock and whores. He would have killed to protect her if Josefina hadn't begged him to spare the man's life. Gar felt his heart swell and at the same time an emptiness wrenched his gut. He wanted her so badly. Gar felt as if he cared about her safety as well as her future. Why in heaven's name did he, when he barely even knew the girl? Nay, nothing could happen between them again. He was falling fast and had to stop it before it was too late.

"My name is Lord Gar, so please don't forget to use my title again," he said, even though his words felt like a stab to his own heart.

She blinked several times and the smile receded from her face.

Damn, why did Gar feel like a bloody, heartless pirate once again?

CHAPTER 11

Josefina stayed in the cabin with Martine and Etta for the trip to Scotland since it continued to rain. She had finally managed to calm down Etta, but it hadn't been easy. The girl was now sleeping peacefully, snug and warm under a blanket.

"That must have been so scary in the tavern," said Martine, sitting down at the table, stacking the dirty dishes. Cup had brought them their food in their cabin today. He also said that Gar instructed them to stay inside the cabin and not to come out until he told them to.

"It was," agreed Josefina, standing across from her. "Thankfully, Lord Gar and Lord Robin came to our rescue."

"Etta said Gar was going to kill the man at the tavern and you stopped him. Is this true?" asked Martine.

"I don't know for sure, but he was very angry and it certainly seemed like it." She took a seat across from Martine. "Lady Martine, I get the impression that Lord Gar doesn't like me anymore."

"Why would you say that?"

"He is purposely keeping his distance from me. He hasn't come to the cabin once since we set sail. Only Cup and Robin were here."

"He's sailing the ship of his dreams. When he gets like this, he ignores everyone so don't take it personally."

"But I saw him on deck. T-Bald is the one sailing the ship right now, not him. Plus, it is no longer raining, yet we're confined to the cabin like prisoners."

"It doesn't bother me," said Martine with a shrug. "I'd rather not be out on the slippery deck and amongst all those smelly men."

"They do stink, don't they?" asked Josefina with a giggle before becoming serious again. "I can't help but wonder if I did something wrong to make Gar, I mean Lord Gar, angry with me."

"Why don't you ask him?" suggested Martine. "That is one way to know for sure."

"Leave the cabin although he warned us to stay here?" She wouldn't mind doing that but thought Martine would want to follow orders from their captain.

"Why not? I'll watch over Etta, so go. Besides, I thought you were in charge on this trip."

"You're right," said Josefina. "No one can tell me not to leave the cabin if I want to. I'm going out there to talk to him right now."

Josefina donned her cloak, feeling a little nervous as she opened the door and stepped out onto the deck. All the crew turned to look at her. She didn't like to be stared at. She closed the door and looked around but didn't see Gar anywhere.

"Are you looking for Lord Gar?" asked Cup, hurrying to her side.

"Yes. Do you know where I can find him? I really need to talk to him."

"Aye. Up there." He looked upward and pointed.

"What?" she asked, not understanding. But then she realized he was pointing at the lookout basket atop the center mast. "Oh, he's way up there. Mayhap I'll just wait until he comes down."

"When he goes up there it is usually to think and relax and look at the water, trying to clear his mind," said Robin, walking up to join them. "Sometimes it is hours or even an entire day before he comes down. If it's anything important, I suggest you go to him."

"Go to him? Up there?" Josefina's eyes opened wide in fear as she looked up the tall mast that seemed to disappear into the clouds.

"Never mind, it's too dangerous for a girl," said Robin. "I never should have suggested it. I'm going to check in on Martine to see if she needs anything." He walked away.

"Are you afraid to go up there?" asked Cup.

Josefina didn't ever want to admit to being afraid. She had learned to hide her fear and to brave anything that came into her life. Admitting she was scared would only make the crew disrespect her even more.

"Nay, of course, I'm not afraid," she said. "I'll just go up there. And talk. To him," she said, wetting her lips with her tongue since her mouth seemed so dry from the salt air that she could barely swallow.

"Do you know how to climb the ratlines?" asked Cup.

"I'm sure I can figure it out. How hard could it be?"

"You'd better leave your cloak here. It'll only get tangled in the lines and cause you to fall. I'll hold it." Cup held out his arms.

"Oh. Of course. That makes sense." Josefina removed her cloak, instantly feeling the cool air against her body. She handed the garment to Cup and slowly walked over to climb the ratlines just to prove she could.

God's eyes, she hoped and prayed that she wouldn't fall.

Gar leaned his body against the side of the lookout basket, holding on to a line above his head that joined others leading to a pole which held the ship's flag. Wanting to get away alone and think, this was the only place he could possibly go. With the wind in his hair and the sea far below him, he felt safe even though he was probably on the most dangerous part of the ship.

He didn't care. Gar liked his solitude. He also wanted to try to clear his head. Thoughts of Josefina kept clouding his judgment. He'd been careless and started to really care about the girl. Normally, that wouldn't be a problem. But because he had direct orders from the king to find and marry a noblewoman, this made it even worse.

If he could just get through this trip, then he'd focus on the king's wishes. But every time he turned around and saw Josefina or heard her voice, something happened to him. This, he decided was the only place he could possibly go where he wouldn't bump into her. Up here he wouldn't find himself wanting to kiss her or caress her soft cheek or feel her silk-spun hair again.

He took a deep breath of the fresh sea air, filling his lungs and clearing his muddled thoughts. Slowly releasing his breath, he finally started to feel in control of himself once again. But then his mind started playing tricks on him because he could have sworn he heard Josefina calling out to him, but he knew it couldn't be so.

"Gar," came her soft voice on the breeze. "Gar, help me, please."

If he wasn't mistaken, it really was her voice and coming from directly below him. He leaned over the edge of the basket, shocked by what he saw. There was Josefina, climbing the lines, making her way up to the basket. Her long, loose hair blew in her eyes and her gown lifted in the wind. Down on the deck was the entire crew, looking up at her, probably trying to see under her dress.

"God's teeth, what in the name of the devil are you doing, Josefina?"

"I— I wanted to talk to you and Cup said you were up here." She gripped the lines so tightly that her fingers turned white. She looked down and gasped. "Oh, this is so high up. Too high. I feel like I'm going to slip and fall."

"Now is a fine time to think about that," he griped, putting one leg over the basket.

"What are you doing?" she asked, her frightened eyes silently telling him how scared she really was.

"I'm coming down there to get you," he told her, starting his descent. He got to her quickly, putting one arm around her waist, grabbing on to the lines on the other side of her. "Don't worry, I've got you. I won't let you fall."

"I don't think I should have attempted this," she said in a shaky voice.

"Nay, you shouldn't have. But now that you are almost there, I'll take you to the top."

"Nay. I think I want to go back down, Gar. I'm scared."

She never seemed to want to admit anything frightened her, so if she just said this aloud, he realized she truly must be scared.

"Trust me, sweetheart. I'll help you, and you won't fall. Once you get to the basket, you'll see how beautiful it is up here. Now release your grip and grab the lines higher. Just take it slow and one foot at a time."

Slowly, she let him guide her until he had brought her to the lookout basket and helped her climb inside. He lowered himself into the basket after her, the small space pushing them close together. God's eyes, her body being pressed up against his felt good. Damned good.

"You're shivering," he said, putting his arms around her holding her back up against his chest.

"Y-yes," she said. "C-cup t-told me not to wear my cloak or I'd get t-tangled and f-fall."

"And he was right," Gar told her.

The wind pushed at them and the fierce waves crashed against the ship causing it to list one way and then the other. Being so high up, the motion seemed enhanced. Gar was used to it, but Josefina wasn't. Her fingers dug into his arms and her eyes closed.

"Oh, I think I am going to be sick," she told him.

"No, you're not. Now, just relax. Take a deep breath of the fresh sea air. Be one with the wind and the water."

"I don't think I can."

"Try it. Take a deep breath and hold it."

She did as he instructed.

"Now release it slowly, along with any fear," he told her.

She released her breath and her body stopped shaking.

"Good. Now, open your eyes and look at the beautiful view. This is breathtaking and something you may never have the chance to see again."

"I don't want to." She still gripped him tightly, keeping her eyes closed.

"Josefina, don't you trust me? I've got you. I promise I won't let you fall."

It took her a minute, but then finally, very slowly, she opened her eyes. She instantly looked down instead of out at the water and gasped once again. "We are so high up! Too high."

"Don't look down," he told her. "Look up at the clouds and sky instead."

As soon as she did what he asked, she seemed to calm down. He leaned in closer and whispered into her ear. "Isn't nature wonderful?"

"I— I suppose so," she said, still not sounding as enthused about it as he did.

"You have to admit that it is truly amazing up here."

"Yes. Yes, it is," she said, finally taking a good look around. "I guess I can see why you like it so much. Even though, I feel better with my feet on the deck."

He chuckled lowly and turned her around to face him. "What is it that was so important that you had to risk breaking your neck climbing the ratlines to find me?"

"I wanted to ask you what I did to disappoint you." Her eyes shyly stared up at him. They looked wet either from the wind or possibly because she was holding back tears.

"What? You didn't disappoint me. Why on earth would you say such a thing?" He couldn't help himself. He reached out and cupped her chin in his palm, feeling her velvety soft skin. "You could never disappoint me, Josefina."

"When we first met you didn't seem to like me much."

"Nor did you like me, either."

"Well, I've changed my mind about you. I saw a deep, sensitive side of you that I think you usually hide from others. I decided I like it."

He chuckled again. "Did you, now? Well, I thought you were nothing but a woman who wanted to rule over a man which is unheard of. Now, I realize you were only trying to maintain control of your late husband's business. That is not an easy thing for a woman to do."

"I discovered that soon enough." She flashed him a quick smile. "I'm determined to carry on alone, but it is getting harder and harder with each passing day."

"Would it help if I told you that I thought you were doing a fine job at handling things on your own?"

"Truly?" Hope and gratitude filled her eyes. "Do you mean that?" She blinked twice in succession.

"Yes, I do, Josefina. You are a strong woman. Although a little bossy at times, I like a challenge."

"So do I." She blushed shyly. The ship listed again and she reached out and grabbed him. "Oh!"

"You're fine," he told her, pulling her up against his chest. She leaned her head against him and he smoothed back her long hair.

"What is going to happen once we finish the trip in Scotland?" she asked him.

"I thought you had a trade to do overseas in Denmark."

"I've decided I don't want to travel overseas. That was what Donald and Clovis did, but I don't want to do it. I want to travel along the coast only. I'm going to tell the crew that after the trade fair in Scotland, our trip is over and we'll head back to Hythe."

"Indeed?" he asked with a raised brow. "I was rather looking forward to taking this phenomenal ship out on the open sea."

"You really do love sailing, don't you?"

"More than you know."

"Then after we return, you can take the *Lady Josefina* wherever you want."

"What do you mean?" he asked.

"I'm going to talk with my brother-by-marriage and suggest we sell the ship, but first I allow you to take it on a journey."

"Sell it? Why?"

"It's too big of a ship for a trade merchant and you know it. The only reason it is this size is because Donald wanted a ship that was bigger and better than the others."

"How will you carry on your business without it?" asked Gar, sad to hear she wanted to get rid of something that Gar would love to own.

"I'll convince Clovis to get a smaller ship and stick to the coast. I know he never liked being away from his family long so he'll most likely agree to my suggestion."

"I see," he said, trying to make sense of this all.

"What about you? What will you do once we return?" she asked him.

"I don't want to think about that right now," he said, dreading the minute he was back and banned from the water.

"Well, what do you want to think about right now?" she asked, staring at his mouth.

"How about this?" he asked, doing the exact thing he was trying to refrain from doing. He pressed his lips up to hers in a deep, long, meaningful kiss. Her body seemed to relax in his embrace. With his touch, Josefina no longer seemed to be frightened of being up so high over the water.

"I like that," she said. "Can we do it again?"

"You know how hard it is for me to say no?"

"Does that mean no?"

"I didn't say that." This time, as he kissed her, he let his hands wander. Skimming downward, he trailed his fingers along her sleek, long neck, stopping to cup her breast. She pushed up against him, seeming to want more. Lost in the moment, Gar leaned over and ran his tongue along her cleavage which caused her to gasp aloud. Then, he slipped his hand into her bodice, flicking his thumb over her nipple, making it to go taut.

"What if someone sees us?" she asked in a breathy whisper, doing nothing to stop him, which told him she wanted him to continue.

"Who is going to see us all the way up here?" he asked, pushing her bodice to the side to expose one of her breasts. His eyes interlocked with hers and he saw lust fill her as much as it did him. Then he lowered his mouth to her nipple.

Josefina couldn't believe what she was doing. Foreplay atop a mast in a lookout basket had to be the most exciting thing she would ever do in her life. Not used to foreplay since Donald never took the time to ready her, she relished each flick of Gar's tongue over her skin. His hand on her breast felt like fire. Her breathing deepened, only managing to make her chest heave in and out. And when he closed his mouth over her nipple and used his tongue to arouse her, she cried out.

"Ooooh," she moaned, arching her back, pushing her breast farther into his mouth. Then he suckled her like a babe and she felt an immediate wave of heat quicken between her thighs.

"What are you feeling?" he asked her.

"I feel aroused. I feel a heat between my legs."

"I'd like to feel that too." He gripped the bottom of her gown and pulled upward. His hand snaked underneath and he cupped her womanhood, making her feel so alive and sexy that if there had been room in the basket, she would have thrown him down and jumped atop him.

"Captain? Are you up there? It is your turn at the helm," called out Hothead Harry. "What is going on up there? What are you doing?"

"Never mind," Gar called down to Harry. Then he was back to caressing her cheek once more. "I'm sorry, Josefina. I would love to stay and continue this, but I need to go down now," he said, kissing her on the mouth once more.

The cool air rushed against her bare breast but he pulled her gown back into place and covered her back up.

"Of course, I understand," she told him. "You are the captain and it is your duty," she said, sad to see this come to an end.

"I will help you down," he told her, and she felt his heart beating rapidly against her chest. "It's getting dark anyway.

It's not safe for you to be up here. But I am glad you got to experience something new today."

"More than one thing," she said with a smile, only hoping they could continue this at a later time, because she was far from being finished.

CHAPTER 12

"Why are you so quiet?" Robin asked Gar later that day on the sterncastle. Robin sat atop a barrel cutting an apple with his dagger. "Is something bothering you?"

Gar was at the helm. The rain had stopped but it was still a cloudy and dreary day. Since they left in the middle of the day, they'd have to spend one more night on the water before they made it to their destination of Dunbar, Scotland.

"What's bothering me is that you are here asking me silly questions when you were hired to protect the women."

"Hired, did you say?" Robin looked up, shoving a piece of apple into his mouth, chewing while he spoke. "I didn't know you were actually paying me to be here."

"I'm not."

"Point taken, then why I'm sitting here instead of standing at the cabin door on guard duty."

"You should be watching over them. I don't trust the crew around them."

"My, someone is grouchy today." Robin ate another slice of apple. "And for your information, I've got Cup watching the cabin door. Not to mention, I can keep an eye on it from here."

"Mmmph," grunted Gar, his mind far too preoccupied to even enjoy sailing such a grand ship.

"Cousin, you are normally smiling when you're at the helm. Right now, you don't even look like you're enjoying it at all."

"I've got other things on my mind."

"Things?" Robin chuckled and continued chewing. "Don't you mean a certain lovely widow?"

"I don't know what you're talking about." Gar stared straight ahead, occasionally glancing at his compass and then down to the deck where the crew was standing around talking. "Get to work swabbing the deck," he called down to the them. "Bosun, you'll be doing it yourself if I don't see that deck cleaned."

"Aye, Cap'n. I'll handle the crew," shouted Crusty Rusty, who was in charge of the crew and the cleanliness of the ship.

"Solobow, I want that rigging checked too," he shouted. "There seems to be a rip in the main sail that needs repair. If I have to come down there, I swear you'll all be sorry."

"Aye, Cap'n," shouted Solobow,

"We're working on it, Captain," spat Harry.

"Calm down, Gar," said Robin. "You sound as if you're going to bite off someone's head.

"This trip isn't turning out at all as I expected."

"It's Josefina, right?" Robin stood up, tossing the apple core over the side into the water. "She's got you hot and bothered." He cleaned his dagger on his tunic and replaced the blade in his weaponbelt.

"Can I ask you something, Robin?"

"Ask away. I'm all ears." Robin smiled and held up his open palms.

Still steering the ship, Gar continued looking out over the water as he talked.

"How did you know that Sage was the right girl for you?"

"What do you mean?"

"I mean, was there a sign that you'd end up marrying her? How did you know you were in love?"

"Ah, it's just as I thought. You are falling fast for Josefina when you know you are expected to marry a noblewoman."

"I've got my orders from the king, and I'll follow them."

"Of course, you will. Because you want to do the right thing and you want people to accept you."

Gar slowly turned to look at his cousin. "Is that wrong?" he asked softly.

"Nay. Not at all," said Robin. "That is, unless a certain woman has stolen your heart and you've led her on to believe there might be more between you someday."

"I didn't mean to lead her on," said Gar. "It just might have... happened."

"You know you can be with her if you want. After all, most of your cousins and even your sister have married from below the salt, so it's not like it can't happen."

"If I ever want to sail again, it can't happen. King Edward has made that more than clear. If I want to be accepted and not called a pirate for the rest of my life, I have to do this."

"Then do it," said Robin with a shrug. "Marry the next noblewoman you see and all your worries will be over."

"I can't."

"Why not?"

"I don't want to hurt Josefina. She's been through so much lately. She's all alone and needs me."

"Hah!" said Robin, waving his hand through the air. "Josefina is a lot like my sister. Too damned headstrong and determined to do what she wants. The girl will be fine without you. I honestly think she'd succeed, even if she never married again."

Gar should have been relieved to hear this, but instead it made him feel even worse. At least when he held the notion that Josefina needed him, it gave him more reason to go against his orders. It made him want to risk losing everything he loved, meaning sailing and being on the water.

Something drew his eyes downward. The cabin door was open and Josefina and Martine were talking with Harry.

"What the hell is going on down there?" he asked aloud. "I don't want Hothead Harry anywhere near the women."

"What?" Robin stretched his neck to see the women and Harry in a conversation. "Where is Cup? He's supposed to be watching them."

"Dammit, Robin. Do your job or I will. T-Bald, to the helm. Now!" Gar shouted.

"Aye, Cap'n." T-Bald hurried as fast as his old legs could carry him, taking the steps to the sterncastle two at a time. At least this was one man Gar totally trusted.

"Keep us on course," instructed Gar, handing the compass to T-Bald. Gar hurried down the steps with Robin right behind him.

"You didn't have to leave the helm," Robin told him.

"Someone's got to watch over the women."

"They're on a ship. There's nowhere to go. They're safe I tell you."

"Get back to your post, Harry," said Gar, stopping at the door to the cabin.

"I'm only trying to help the ladies," said the man.

"I'm here now. Go!"

"A little cantankerous today, are we?" mumbled Harry over his shoulder as he left.

"Etta is missing," said Martine with worry in her voice.

"We can't find her anywhere," added Josefina. "I hope she didn't fall overboard. I'm so worried about her."

"How the hell can she be missing?" asked Gar. "I thought she was in the cabin with the two of you."

"She was sleeping behind the curtain, but must have sneaked out of the cabin when we weren't looking," replied Martine.

"This is horrible," said Josefina. "We've got to find her."

"She's a stowaway, so mayhap she's down in the hold looking for something to eat again. I'll check," said Robin.

"We'll check the galley," said Martine, speaking of her and Josefina.

"I'd rather you stay in the cabin," said Gar. "I'll go."

"This is my ship and I'll go wherever I like," snapped Josefina.

That took him aback. Even after the intimate time together they'd spent in the lookout basket, Josefina was back to ordering him around again. He supposed it was because she was worried about the girl so he let it go.

Gar let out a deep breath. "All right, then. Just stay out in the open where I can see you," he said. Then he turned and addressed the crew. "The young girl is missing. Everyone look for her," he called out.

"The stowaway?" asked Two-Spit. "Good. Mayhap she fell overboard."

"Or mayhap one of you pushed her," snapped Gar.

"Nay! Do you really think they did?" asked Josefina, very upset by his comment.

"Nay, I don't really believe that," Gar said, just to calm her down. "I'll check the forecastle and sterncastle," said Gar, heading away.

Everyone searched the ship, but no one found her. Just when Gar started worrying that the girl really did fall overboard, something made him look up – the one place they hadn't checked.

"Gar, no one can find her. What are we going to tell the girls?" asked Robin.

"Nothing yet. I have one more place to look and I have a funny feeling I'm about to find her." Grabbing hold of the ratlines, Gar climbed quickly to the same lookout basket that he and Josefina had been in earlier. He pulled himself up and looked over the edge of the basket to see the young girl hunkered down inside. "I thought I'd find you here."

"Lord Gar!" said Etta, sounding surprised to see anyone up there.

Gar hoisted himself into the basket with her. "Why did you leave the cabin without telling anyone where you were going?"

"What difference does it make? No one cares." Etta's expression was defiant.

"That's not true," he said.

"Who cares about me?" she asked, standing up, looking out over the edge of the basket. "The entire crew wants to throw me overboard."

"The crew cares about no one but themselves. Martine and Josefina are very worried about you."

"What about you?" she asked, crossing her arms over her chest. "Do you care what happens to me?"

This wasn't at all what Gar expected. Why did this girl have to ask such a question? He felt a knot twist in his gut. Wasn't it bad enough that he already admitted to Robin that he had feelings for Josefina? Now, he was supposed to say he cared about a stowaway child that he didn't even know?

"Of course, I care about you, Etta," he heard himself say, realizing he only said it because he didn't want the girl to think he was some kind of heartless ogre.

"You do?" she asked, a smile turning up the corners of her mouth. "No one ever cares what happens to me." Tears formed in her eyes.

"What happened to your parents?" he asked her.

"My father was killed by a bandit on the road when I was three. My mother had to raise me by herself."

"Tell me about your mother," he said. "Did she have a way to make money?"

"She didn't want to whore herself out for coin, so she did something just as bad. She took care of those with grave diseases. Because of it, she got sick and died when I was ten."

"Ten?" Again, that surprised him. "So, you've been on your own for the last three years?"

"Not really. I told Josefina I'm thirteen, but I'm really only a tall eleven-year-old."

"Eleven?" Gar dragged his hand through his long hair. So, Etta really was only a child as Josefina had said. "So, you lied?"

"I had to." Etta looked out at the water. "If people thought I was in my teens, at least I'd have a fighting chance of being accepted. No one wants a child to look after. I wanted to prove I was worthy of helping out if someone ended up taking me in."

"You're only eleven? Really?" he asked just to make sure, feeling even more responsible for her now.

She looked at him with wide eyes and nodded silently.

"Gar!" shouted Robin from the deck. "What are you doing up there? This is no time to hide away. You're needed down here."

"Stop your complaining," he yelled over the side of the basket. "I found the girl. I'll bring her down."

"Oh, thank goodness," shouted Josefina, standing with Martine and Robin, wringing her hands in worry.

"Etta, you've got to stop this nonsense of disappearing. You are causing unwanted distractions and I can't have that on my ship."

"I thought this was Josefina's ship," said the girl, driving that blade right through his heart again. Actually, the blade was already there and the girl's words just twisted it harder.

"You know what I mean. I'm captain, and I command you to stay with the women and not wander off anymore. Do you hear me? This ship isn't safe for a young girl. Or the women, for that matter," he said looking down at Martine and Josefina. "I don't want to find out something bad has happened to any of you."

"So, you do care about me after all!" Her face lit up in

excitement. It meant the world to the girl that someone cared about her, and he understood why. He had a mother, but when he was young, he had always been raised by whores and left ashore while his mother and the man he thought was his grandfather sailed the seas. It wasn't a good feeling in the least. Everyone needed to have that feeling of belonging somewhere.

"When I was young, I was left behind and felt like an orphan although I wasn't," he told Etta.

"Where were your parents?" she asked.

"My father was dead. My mother and grandfather went out sailing the seas without me."

"Is that why you like sailing so much now?" came the wise voice of youth. "Because you never got to do it when you were young?"

"I— I guess so," he said, never really realizing this before now. "Sometimes when we want something so badly, it's all we think about. All we know is that something is missing in our lives even if we don't really understand what it is."

"I know what's missing in my life," said Etta. "I don't want to be alone, Captain. I'm afraid of being alone. That is one of the reasons why I sneaked aboard your ship to begin with. I just want to be around people."

"Then why are you up here now all by yourself?"

"I saw you and Josefina up here earlier and I was curious what you were looking at. I wanted to see for myself."

Gar chuckled, glad the girl didn't really know what he and Josefina were doing up here.

"I want a family more than anything in life." Her bottom lip stuck out in a pout.

"I understand," said Gar, not sure what to say to make

things better for the girl. "I'll tell you what. Once we reach land, I'll take you anywhere you want to go. Just please don't sneak off by yourself again."

"I'd like that," said Etta. "Can Josefina come with us? I really like her. She's so nice. Don't you agree?"

He did agree, and that was the problem. Spending time with Josefina was only going to make things harder for both of them when he left her after this trip to find a noble-woman to marry. "Yes, Josefina is nice," he said, looking down at Josefina who was looking up at him from the deck, waiting for him to bring Etta down. He started thinking again about how it felt to hold Josefina in his arms. It warmed his heart each time he kissed her. Damn, he was going to miss her. "Too damned nice," he said, still speaking of Josefina. He put one leg over the edge of the lookout basket, getting ready to climb down the lines.

Gar had planned to stay away from Josefina as much as possible until they returned to Hythe. But now, wanting Etta to like him, he'd just promised the girl that he, along with Josefina, would spend time with her once they reached Scotland. Was it an accident that he'd agreed? Or did he secretly want more time with Josefina before he had to leave her forever and is that why he made the promise? Suddenly, he wasn't sure anymore. Everything in his life was changing so fast that he wondered if fate had taken a turn for the better or was it for the worse? He supposed he'd just have to keep his promise to Etta and spend time with the girl along with Josefina and find out for sure. Then again, somehow he already knew the answer.

CHAPTER 13

"Drop the anchor and lower the sails," Gar called out from the helm a few hours later. "We're stopping here for the night."

"What? Why?" Hothead Harry bolted up the steps. "We can sail into the night," said Harry. "It'll get us to Scotland faster. Why are we stopping?"

"We're stopping because I said so," answered Gar, really only wanting to slow down the trip so he had more time to spend with Josefina. "I prefer daylight to see where I'm sailing. Now, watch the helm until the crew carries out all the orders." He walked away before Harry could object to his decision again.

Even though Robin swore he'd be keeping a close eye on the women, Gar wanted to make sure they were all right. He made his way to the cabin and entered to find Robin leaning back on two legs of a chair, sleeping with his back against the wall. His loud snores filled the room. The women were all there and safe, but no thanks to his cousin.

"Wake up!" he spat, using his foot to kick out the legs of the chair, sending Robin sprawling across the floor.

"What? Who? How?" Robin shouted, scrambling to his feet, pulling his sword from his scabbard.

"Put away the blade before you hurt one of the ladies," he told his cousin.

"Gar!" Josefina jumped up from her seat at the table, happy to see him. But before she could approach him, Etta ran over, wrapping her arms around him, giving him a big hug. Josefina stood there with her mouth hanging open. "My turn," she said, gently pushing the young girl aside and giving Gar a big hug right there in front of everyone.

"Whatever is going on here, don't expect me to do that, because I'm not," said Martine with a roll of her eyes.

"Oh, Gar. Good, you're here," said Robin, sheathing his sword and yawning.

"We'll be at Dunbar early tomorrow morning," Gar announced, feeling uncomfortable since Josefina still had her arms around him. He gently pushed her arms down and stepped away. "Tonight, only the women will stay in the cabin. Robin will sleep outside the door."

"Outside the door? On the deck?" griped Robin. "I'm a noble and at least deserve a pallet."

"If you're outside the door, then hopefully you'll at least wake up if anyone enters or exits," Gar told him.

"I want to spend tomorrow walking in the hills," Etta blurted out. "We can bring a basket of food to eat in a field of heather. That's what I want to do."

"What?" said Gar, trying to figure out what the girl was rambling on about.

"You promised you were going to take me wherever I

wanted once we reached Scotland," said Etta with a new glow of life about her. "Well, that's the first thing I want to do."

"You promised her that?" asked Robin, looking at Gar as if he thought he were addled.

"Well, I might have— I mean, yes. I did."

"I see." Josefina seemed angry with him for some reason.

"And he promised that you'd come too," said Etta, taking Josefina by the hand.

"Oh, he did?" Josefina's face softened and she looked up at Gar with those beautiful ochre eyes that drew him in. God, he wanted to caress her cheek again and taste her lips pressed up against his. "That is nice, however, I'm afraid I can't come with you," she told Etta.

"What?" Gar's heart jumped. The only reason he'd agreed to such an absurd thing was because he thought Josefina would be with them. He didn't know the first thing about children and didn't want to have to care for the girl alone. God's eyes, this couldn't be happening. "You have to go too. Why can't you come with us?" he demanded to know, his voice sounding a bit gruffer than he'd intended.

"I can't join you because I'll need to be tending my stalls at the trade fair. You know that. I have a business to run." Josefina looked at him with a bit of caution if he wasn't mistaken. He wondered if mayhap he'd scared her. He didn't want a fight on his hands, but he also wasn't going to take the child anywhere by himself. He had to think of an excuse quickly to get himself out of this mess.

"I'm sure the crew could cover the stalls for a while," Gar told Josefina, still trying to get her to join them.

"Mayhap, but they don't know the first thing about selling silk to the nobles."

"Martine can do that," said Gar quickly.

"Oh, I'd love to help out, however, I promised Lark I'd meet her," Martine told them. "We already have plans. I'm sorry I can't help you again at the trade fair," Martine told Josefina.

"It's all right. Family is important. Spend time with your cousin," said Josefina sweetly. "I'll manage."

"Well, mayhap Robin can—" Gar started saying, but Robin cut him off.

"Nay. I'll be escorting my sister to meet up with Lady Lark and Lord Dustin," said Robin. "Sorry. Can't do it."

"And neither should you," Josefina told him. "I appreciate all the help you've already given me, but nobles shouldn't be behind the tables selling wares. It's not right for someone of your status. I don't expect any of you to do it. I'll handle things myself, don't worry."

"I guess it'll just be me and you, then," said Etta, smiling at Gar. Damn, he didn't want to disappoint the child, but neither did he want to have to tend to her when he should be in the tavern drinking with the other nobles. None of this was right.

"Perhaps we can do it another time, Etta. When Josefina can join us," suggested Gar.

"Oh. You don't want to be with me. I understand." The young girl pouted and disappeared behind the hanging curtain.

"Gar," whispered Josefina. "Just take her wherever she wants to go. If you upset her, she'll run away again and I don't have the time to be searching for her. None of us do."

"Yes, dear Cousin," said Robin, laughing. "You made a promise to the girl, now keep it."

"But I can't!" protested Gar, lowering his voice so Etta wouldn't hear him. "I don't know the first thing about tending to children. Please, one of you has got to help me out."

"You can do it," said Josefina, sounding as if she were trying to be supportive, but it came across as condescending in his mind.

"Don't go breaking girls' hearts," Robin warned him with a wink and a chuckle. Gar knew damned well he was really talking about Josefina.

"I'm going to check with Wilkens about the meal. Everyone, be on the deck in half an hour or go hungry!" Gar left the cabin, cursing himself for having had a heart to begin with. If he had been his usual self, he wouldn't be saddled with a job like this. The only thing he wanted was to spend time with Josefina. Instead, he'd be spending time with a child who seemed to suddenly idolize him since he paid her a bit of attention.

Gar closed the door behind him, wanting this trip to be over and done. Never in his life had he wished for a sailing trip to be over before today. He had started out excited to be captaining the ship of his dreams. But with not one, not two, but three girls aboard, his dream was quickly turning into an endless nightmare.

～

"I think I'd better talk with Gar. Lord Gar," Josefina corrected herself, heading for the cabin door.

"Josefina, you two have had intimate relations so I think it is fine to address Gar without using his title," Martine told her.

"They did? How intimate?" asked Robin.

"Brother! That is not something you ask a woman. It is none of your business," scolded Martine.

"Well, you are the one who said it, not me," answered Robin, "Wait for me. I'll escort you, Josefina." Robin hurried out the door with her.

"Thank you, but I don't need an escort," Josefina told him kindly. "I'm on the ship and I know the crew. Nothing is going to happen to me."

"I know. I just wanted to speak to you in private," said Robin.

"Oh? Whatever for?" she asked.

"I know my cousin has strong feelings for you."

Josefina felt the heat rising to her face. "Did he tell you that?" She hoped Gar hadn't told Robin what else they'd done in the lookout basket.

"He didn't need to say it. I know him well enough that I can read him like a book."

"What are you saying?" She felt confused.

"I am saying that if you don't take the time to be with Gar in Scotland, you may never see him again."

"But I have a business to run. I can't help it."

"He's falling in love with you, but he is still adamant about following the king's command and marrying a noblewoman."

"Oh." Her heart sank. "I understand. It is what is expected of him as a noble."

"Nay, you don't understand. Don't you see? I married

from below the salt and so did four of my cousins. There is no reason to believe that Gar won't follow in those same footsteps."

"Are you saying he wants to marry me?" She held her breath, waiting for Robin's answer.

"Nay, that's not what I'm saying at all."

"Oh, I see."

"You don't understand. I am saying that Gar doesn't know he wants to marry you yet, but I for one, know that he does."

"How so?" She cocked her head, trying to understand how Robin knew these things before she did.

"God's eyes, wench. Think about it. He is a man whose only passion before meeting you was sailing and having a life on the water."

"Isn't that still his passion?" she asked innocently.

"It sure as hell didn't seem that way when I saw him at the helm earlier. He was in such deep thought that he could have been driving a team of horses over land rather than sailing a ship on the ocean and he wouldn't have known the difference."

"Does this have anything to do with the fact that he told Etta he'd spend time with her and that I would be with them?"

"It has everything to do with that. Don't you see?"

"He was trying to make an orphan happy."

"He was trying to find a way to be with you without coming out and saying he wanted to spend time with you."

"Huh?"

"If he came right out and asked you to spend time with

him, he'd feel as if he were disobeying a direct order from the king."

"But he wouldn't. I mean, we'd only be spending time together, that's all."

"And that is why you need to go with him and Etta. If you object, there will be no chance in hell of ever winning him over a noblewoman."

"Does he know a noblewoman that he wants to marry?"

"Of course not. He doesn't want to marry anyone."

She frowned. "Then what exactly are you telling me to do, Lord Robin? You make no sense at all."

"I'm telling you to get busy and change Gar's mind."

"Change his mind? You want me to deceive him?"

"Not at all. I want you to have the chance you two deserve because I can see it as plain as day that you belong together."

"You're not just saying this because you married a girl who wasn't noble and you want him to make the same mistake?"

"Mistake?" Now Robin looked surprised. "Mayhap I was wrong about you. Forgive me, I thought you had feelings for Gar."

"I do."

"Then don't let him marry a noblewoman whom he doesn't even know and certainly won't love."

"I don't want to take the chance away from him to ever sail the sea again."

Robin blew air from his mouth and swiped his hand through the air. "Like you have any control where that is concerned."

"You really think I should find a way to go with him and Etta when we reach Scotland?"

"Nay, forget it."

"Nay? But I thought you just said that—"

"I think you should find a way to spend time with him and dump Etta. The child is only going to get in your way."

"Mayhap you are right."

The door to the cabin opened and Martine and Etta walked out.

"Do what you want," said Robin. "This is none of my concern. I just wanted to see you two as happy and Sage and I are right now. Good luck. I am going to find some food," Robin said the last part loud enough for the women to hear him.

"I'll come with you, Lord Robin." Etta ran to his side. "If you don't like what Whiney Wilkens made, I'll show you where to find the good stuff in the hold." Etta actually giggled. It did Josefina's heart good to hear the girl laugh.

"You'd better hold on to Robin so you don't fall," suggested Martine, getting a dirty look from her brother.

"Let's go," said Robin impatiently as he walked away with Etta clinging to his sleeve like a lifeline.

Martine giggled behind her hand as they left.

"You wanted Etta to go with him, didn't you?" asked Josefina.

"He's been too comfortable this entire trip," said Martine. "Let my brother start figuring out just what it's like to have a child since his baby will be born soon."

"You're enjoying this, aren't you?" asked Josefina.

"You might be right. We always teased each other

growing up, but since we're adults we don't have that kind of fun anymore. This more than makes up for it, though."

The women walked slowly toward the galley.

"Lady Martine, do you think I have a chance at all of ending up with Gar?"

"I don't see why not. I mean, I've seen crazier things happen."

"Like what?" she asked.

"What I mean is, you are not a noble, but you are successful and you do have money. That is more than I can say for my cousin Rook's wife, Rose, who was a gardener. Don't get me wrong, I adore her. I am just saying you are closer to being to Gar's status than Rose was with Rook. And they are happily married and everything worked out just fine."

"I don't know why you are talking about marriage. Things are happening so fast that my head is spinning." Josefina, held her hand to her forehead.

"Then slow down, but don't miss the opportunity to get to know each other while on this trip."

"That is the same thing Robin told me."

"Really? Hmmm. Then mayhap my brother isn't the mindless knave I always thought him to be."

"Come on, ladies, the food is gettin' cold and we're all waitin' for you to eat first because it's the captain's orders," complained Whiney Wilkens.

"I say we eat without them," yelled out Two Spit Sam, spitting on the deck.

"Stop the damned spitting or I'll make you clean the deck with your tongue," ground out Gar, still in a foul mood.

Josefina smiled. It wasn't so bad letting Gar command

the crew after all, she supposed. She really liked Gar and wanted more than anything to get to know him better like Martine and Robin had suggested. Yes, she decided. She would find a way to be with Gar and Etta tomorrow after all. Because if she didn't, she would probably regret it for the rest of her life.

◆

CHAPTER 14

"Land ho!" Gar called out, as they reached the shores of Dunbar, Scotland. "Lower those sails and drop anchor," he called out. "The docks are full and we'll have to stay out here." He'd had to anchor the ship in the waters off the docks and they'd need to take shuttle boats to and from the shore since the area was so crowded. This was only a small wharf and not at all the size of the one in Scarborough. He supposed it was because of the trade fair going on that they were filled.

The crew busily prepared the ship for mooring and Gar headed down from the sterncastle to find Solobow.

"Anchor is dropped," said Solobow, hurrying over to meet him.

"Good. Now help Harry and Rusty ready the shuttles to take us as well as the cargo to shore."

"Aye, Cap'n."

"Gar," called out Josefina picking up the hem of her

gown and sidestepping several crewmembers, making her way over to him.

"You should really call me Lord Gar around the men," he reminded her.

"Yes, you're right. I'm sorry, Lord Gar. I won't make that mistake again."

"We can't get near the wharf to dock, so we'll have to load the cargo into shuttles and have the men take it to the trade fair for you from here."

"Yes. Two-Spit will be handling that for me."

"What? Why? Don't you think you should be giving the orders?"

"I'm not taking the silks and cloth today. As a matter of fact, I'm not going to bring a lot of cargo ashore."

"Why not?" he asked, winding up a line as he spoke. "You are the one always saying that the business cannot suffer."

"I am only bringing items that the crew can handle and sell for me."

"The crew?" Gar hung up the skein of rope. "Why does it sound as if you won't be with them?"

"I won't," she said. "Or, not today, at least. I have something more important to do."

"More important than making a sale?"

"Yes. I will be walking barefoot through a field of heather with a basket of food over my arm."

"Josefina? What are you saying?"

"I'm coming with you and Etta today."

"You are?" Gar was ecstatic to hear this. "Great! What made you change your mind?"

"I know how much it'll mean to Etta. I don't want to disappoint her."

"Is that the only reason?" A strand of hair blew in her eyes and Gar quickly reached out and brushed it back behind her ear.

"There might be another reason." She looked up at him and smiled in a sultry manner.

"Don't be doing that here." He pulled back his hand and looked the other way, wetting his lips with his tongue. "You keep that up and we'll never get off the ship. Instead, I'll throw you over my shoulder and bring you back to the cabin and have my way with you."

"My lord! I cannot believe you just said that." Josefina was smiling and didn't seem angry or insulted by his remark at all. In fact, she almost seemed to like it.

"I can't believe you didn't object." He smiled back, purposely letting his eyes drop to her cleavage to see how she'd react. She smiled once again.

"All right, you two. None of that in front of the child," said Robin, walking over with Martine and Etta right behind him. "Is our shuttle ready to bring us to shore?"

"Solobow, is there a shuttle ready?" Gar called out.

"Aye, Captain. I will row it myself."

"Let's go," said Gar, guiding Josefina with his hand on the small of her back. Once they were dropped off at shore, Solobow took the shuttle back to the ship to help the rest of the crew load the cargo and bring it to the fair. "Keep an eye on the men and don't let Harry or Two-Spit handle any money," Gar called out after the man. Solobow nodded and rowed back to the ship.

"I hope I'm not making a mistake sending the crew in my place," said Josefina.

"Is T-Bald going to the trade fair too?" asked Gar.

"He is," she answered. "I gave him the money to pay rent for the stalls."

"That, at least, makes me feel a little better."

"Lord Gar, we need to find some food so we can take it with us to a field of heather," said Etta impatiently.

Gar looked back to Solobow who was too far away now to hear him. "I guess now isn't a good time to think we should have brought some food from the hold."

"Why don't we go to the Sand Star Inn?" asked Martine. "That is where Lark asked me to meet her."

"It's not far from here," said Robin. "I'll hire someone with a horse and wagon to take us there." He raised his hand in the air to flag someone down.

"Ladies, take a seat," said Gar once the wagon arrived. There was just enough room for two people to sit on the bench seat next to the driver. Gar helped Martine up, and then held out his hand to help Josefina.

Josefina wanted to sit by Gar, so she grabbed a hold of Etta and brought her in front of her. "I'm sure Etta would like to ride up front. I'll sit in the wagon," said Josefina.

"Have it your way." Gar helped Etta get settled and then walked to the back of the wagon with Josefina. Robin was already inside. "Up you go." Gar's hands closed around Josefina's waist, and she reached out and put her hands on his shoulders. She purposely let her fingertips trail down his chest once he seated her atop the hay inside the wagon.

She saw him look up quickly and shoot her a quick grin.

Then he hopped in next to her just as the wagon jolted, heading away.

"Oh!" Josefina wasn't expecting that, and almost fell out of the wagon.

"I'd better hold on to you," said Gar, grabbing her and pulling her up against him. He wrapped his arm around her waist.

"This is nice," she said, already glad she decided to spend the day with Gar.

"I agree." He pulled her closer, quickly kissing her atop her head.

"Was that a kiss I felt?" She looked up into his eyes which were twinkling playfully.

"Nay. I just wanted to sniff your hair."

"Sniff my hair?" She laughed. "You couldn't think of something a little more clever than that to say?"

"I mean it," he said, leaning over and sniffing again. "Your hair smells like flowers. I like that."

Just as they approached the inn, something shot out from under the hay, scaring Josefina.

"Ah!" she cried, leaning up against Gar for protection.

"It's just a cat," said Gar, scooping up a gray, black and white spotted cat from the hay with one hand.

"Oh, is that a cat?" Etta jumped right over the back of the wagon, hurrying over to pet the animal.

"That darned thing is still here?" complained the driver. "I don't want that cat in my wagon. I've gotten rid of it three times now and it keeps coming back here."

"Can I have it?" Etta asked the driver.

"Please do. I want it gone."

"Robin, aren't you going to help me out of the wagon?"

asked Martine. Robin was sleeping and Gar reached out and hit him on the leg.

Robin snorted and sat upright. "Are we there?"

"We are there and I am still waiting," complained Martine.

"I'm coming." Robin hopped over the side of the wagon to help Martine.

"I've always wanted a pet," said Etta, smiling and snuggling her nose up against the cat.

"Don't get too used to that damn thing because you're not bringing it aboard the ship," Gar told her, getting out of the back of the wagon.

"Why not?" asked Etta.

"Yes. Why not?" Josefina echoed as he helped her out, as well.

"Josefina, really? I already have three females aboard and now you want a cat too? Please, don't try my patience that far."

"I promise to watch her closely," said Etta, making Gar snort.

"Another female. It figures. Nay. It'll get under the feet of the crew," he told her.

Josefina noticed the sad look on Etta's face. "What if she promised to keep it in the cabin for the journey?" She made sure to ask Gar, not tell him. This would appeal to his male pride and also hopefully bring them closer together. She kept thinking about what Robin and Martine told her. She had very little time to win Gar over before she'd never see him again.

"Pleeeeease?" asked Etta, holding up the cute cat in front of Gar's face. The animal mewed and nudged Gar's hand.

"Please?" asked Josefina.

"Oh, what the hell. Why not?" Gar scratched the back of his neck. "What's one more mouth to feed?"

"Thank you!" Etta jumped out of the wagon, holding the cat with two hands against her chest.

"Move yer big body, ye, lunk, so I can get through. Ye're blockin' the way!" came a voice from behind Gar.

They all turned to see a blonde Scottish lady standing there holding the hand of a little girl around four years of age. She had blonde hair as well. Behind them was a lord with long dark hair.

"Lark!" cried out Martine from the front of the wagon, running over to them. The women hugged.

"Hello, Cousin Lark," said Gar. "I hear congratulations are in order since you're going to have a baby. Lord Dustin." Gar reached out and shook the man's hand. Robin greeted them as well.

"Thank ye," said Lark. "And I was just jestin' when I called ye a lunk."

"I don't believe it for a moment, but I'll take that as an apology," said Gar.

"Who are they?" asked the little girl with Lark, nodding at Josefina and Etta.

"Florie, that isna nice," said Lark. "She looked at Josefina. "I am Lady Lark and this is my husband, Lord Dustin and my daughter— our daughter, Florie."

"Hello," said Dustin, sounding very friendly.

"This is Josefina, and Etta," Gar introduced them. Josefina stepped forward.

"I am the owner of the ship called the *Lady Josefina*," she explained. "I am a widow taking over my late husband's trade business."

"How old are ye?" Florie asked Etta. "And is that your cat? It's pretty."

"I'm thirteen," said Etta.

Gar cleared his throat.

"I mean, eleven," said Etta shyly, still snugging the cat. "And yes, this is my pet."

"What is the cat's name?" asked Florie, reaching up to pet it.

"It doesn't have a name yet," Etta explained.

"I'll help ye name it. Are ye comin' back to the Sandy Inn with us?"

"It's called Sand Star Inn, sweetheart," her father corrected her.

"Nay, we're going to a field of heather to eat food there with my new cat," said Etta.

"Why don't you invite your cousin and her family to go with us?" Josefina whispered to Gar.

"I think that's a great idea," said Martine, overhearing her. "We can all go. You too, Robin."

Robin grunted and Gar groaned.

"We'll just need to get some food from the inn first," said Josefina, excited to be meeting more of Gar's family. They were all so nice.

"And don't forget plenty of whisky and wine," said Robin.

"Yes. Lots of that," agreed Gar as they headed into the inn with Florie and Etta leading the way.

Before long, they were all piled into a wagon and Dustin drove it up a hill to a field of heather. The day turned out to be nice and the sun was even shining. Everyone chatted happily. The two young girls were even singing. When the cat shrieked loudly as if singing along, everyone started laughing.

"What was that?" asked Josefina.

"It sounded like a shriek," said Robin.

"Like a shrieking banshee," said Gar with a chuckle.

"That's what I'll name her. Banshee," said Etta, holding up the cat that continued to make a lot of noise.

"Great," said Gar. "Now we will have three girls and a shrieking Banshee on our journey. Just what I always wanted aboard my ship."

"Whose ship?" asked Josefina, making Gar groan again.

"Our ship," he said, instead of saying it was hers. Since Josefina liked the idea of something they shared being called theirs, she didn't correct him again.

They piled out of the wagon and the women spread blankets on the ground while the men tended to the horse and brought baskets of food from the wagon.

"I hope we have something for Banshee to eat," said Etta, taking a seat next to her new friend, Florie. Even though the girls weren't that close in age, it seemed as if Etta liked having another child around. She'd started acting her age and Josefina decided that was the best thing for the girl.

The meal was delicious, consisting of cold pork, salted herring, cheese chunks, boiled eggs, and a variety of dried fruits and nuts. There was also plenty of cider and wine. Robin had even somehow managed to secure a bottle of whisky. The alcohol seemed to help relax the men. Josefina found herself relaxing as well, after having one sip of the potent liquid.

"I'll clean up," she said, getting up too fast and feeling dizzy. She reached out to steady herself and almost stepped on the cat. Trying to avoid it, she twisted, ending up falling right on Gar's lap.

"Florie, why dinna ye and yer new friend pick a bouquet of heather to take back to the inn?" said Lark.

"All right. Banshee wants to come with us." Etta got up and scooped up her new pet.

"Etta, you'd better take a few extra herring in case the cat doesn't want to listen to you, then you can lure her back." Gar handed her two leftover salted herrings. Josefina was still on his lap but every time she tried to get up, he held her tighter.

"I'd better go with the girls," said Dustan. "There is a stream up ahead and I don't want them to fall in."

"A stream?" asked Robin. "I'd like to water the horse so I'll come with you."

That left Martine and Lark who were suddenly whispering behind their hands.

"Wait for us," Martine called out. "Lark and I want to help pick flowers."

"Aye," said Lark. "I hope ye two dinna mind stayin' here alone to watch the cart."

"Of course not. Go ahead. I've got it covered." Gar held up the bottle of whisky and then took another sip.

"Would you like more whisky?" asked Gar, holding the bottle up to her.

She didn't want to say no, so she took a small sip and ended up coughing since it was so strong.

"I think you need air," said Gar. "Let me help with that." Pulling her closer to him, still atop his lap, he boldly kissed her right there in the field of heather.

And his kiss lingered, pleasing Josefina. His scent of man and leather filled her senses, with the taste of whisky on his lips making her feel heady. And when his tongue slipped between her lips and filled her mouth, she felt as if she were going to melt.

Reaching up, she put her hands on his shoulders as they continued to kiss. Then, he leaned back, pulling her atop him.

"Gar, what are you doing?" she gasped, wondering how this would look to the rest of their friends. She especially didn't want the children to see this.

"I'm kissing the woman who stole my heart," he said, with a silly grin on his face. "And I'm hoping to do so much more with her too." He reached around her and squeezed her bottom, pulling her up against him even more, enabling her to feel his erection beneath his trews.

It felt so good and she felt herself coming to life, wanting to know Gar intimately in every way. But this wasn't right. Not out here in the open field.

She pushed up to a sitting position, looking at Gar lying there with his long, dark hair sprawled out on the ground. She swore he looked like a pagan god, luring her closer with the way he undressed her with just his eyes.

"I think you've had enough of this for now." She pulled the bottle of whisky from his grip and corked it up. "What is this stuff, anyway? It is the strongest whisky I've ever tasted in my life."

"I don't know. Robin got a hold of it."

"Och, ye found the Mountain Magic," said Lark, returning for her cloak. "Ye'd better watch out with that."

"Mountain Magic?" asked Josefina, not knowing what she meant.

"It's made by my great grandda, Callum MacKeefe," she explained. "He owns the Horn and Hoof Tavern in Glasgow. The whisky brings in good money for our clan."

"Then you'd better take it back," said Josefina, handing her the bottle.

"Why dinna ye keep it. For later." Lark smiled devilishly, donned her cloak and hurried back to the others.

If Josefina knew exactly how dangerous that whisky could be, she never would have agreed to hold on to it.

The day went by quickly, and after the meal and whisky, Gar wasn't much of a help when they returned to the stalls at the trade fair. He sat at the back of one stall, dozing off while Josefina helped the crew make some last minute sales of the day.

"When are we going to head to Denmark?" asked Harry.

"We're not," said Josefina, packing up the rest of the inventory. Since they hadn't brought much ashore and sold most of it today, she decided they'd bring the things back to the ship instead of making the crew sleep here to guard it. Then, in the morning, they could bring more back again. "I don't want to do overseas trades anymore. I was thinking mayhap we'd spend a few more days here and then head on home." She had been having such a good time with Gar's family that she wasn't in a hurry to leave.

"We're not going anywhere," came Gar's sleepy voice from the stall.

"What did you say, Cap'n?" asked Rusty.

"There's a storm on the horizon. It's too dangerous to sail. We'll stay here for at least another few days like Josefina said."

"Yes. Yes, that sounds like a good idea," agreed Josefina, wanting to spend as much time with Gar as possible.

"A storm?" asked Hothead Harry. "There isn't a cloud in the sky."

"Aye," agreed Two-Spit. "And if we wait too long, our contact in Denmark will have left. We can't lose this trade. Denmark is one of our best ports."

"And if we're going to make it there in time, we really need to leave tonight," said Harry.

"Nay," growled Gar. "Josefina doesn't want to go. Besides, it's too dangerous out on the open sea with a storm coming. I won't risk the ship or the lives of the crew." He spoke with his eyes still closed and his arms crossed over his chest.

"I still say we go," protested Harry, not happy with the decision. "Clovis told us we should. We have a standing deal with a merchant over there that will bring us a lot of wealth, but only if we make it there in the next few days. If we miss him, we miss out."

"Then forget it," said Gar. "It'll most likely take a week to cross the North Sea this time of year. And with the storm approaching, we may never make it there at all."

"We've made it across the sea in just a few days before," protested Harry.

"But not from Scotland," Josefina pointed out. "Donald

would cross the channel and travel up north along the shore. Those conditions are quite different."

"Like I said. It's not happening," Gar said, sitting up and looking perturbed.

"Josefina, you aren't going to let him tell you what to do, are you?" asked Hothead, throwing things around in anger. "We need to leave for Denmark. We need that trade."

Josefina felt as if she were in a bad position. She knew how important the Denmark trade would be. It was a yearly deal that had brought her late husband a lot of money. But things were different now. Donald was gone, and she'd made the decision to stop in Dunbar. She also didn't want to do overseas trades anymore. With no experience at all when it came to sailing and the sea, she decided to listen to Gar who knew all about weather conditions on the water.

"Gar is the captain and what he says goes. Now, load up the goods and get them back to the ship," said Josefina.

"I don't want to hear another word about leaving for Denmark," Gar told the crew. "Savvy?"

"Savvy?" repeated Josefina in shock, wondering how that pirate word slipped out of his mouth. She figured it must be the whisky making him silly.

"Aye, Cap'n," said T-Bald who was there as well. "You heard the captain. Get these things back to the ship. Go!"

The crew begrudgingly did as told.

"Gar, we need to go back to the inn for the night," said Josefina. "Lady Lark told me they secured two rooms. One for the men and another for the women."

"I don't like this," mumbled Gar as they headed back to the inn.

Once inside, they joined the others at a table. They'd already ordered food and Josefina and Gar joined them.

"I canna wait to birth my bairn," said Lady Lark holding her hand over her belly.

"When is the baby due?" asked Josefina, eating a spoonful of pottage. Gar ate as well, but was very quiet.

"She's got a long way to go yet," Lark's husband answered for her.

"I want a brother," said Florie.

"You do?" asked Josefina in surprise. "I thought every girl wanted a sister."

"I want Etta for my sister. She's nice," said Florie, handing a piece of fish to the cat that was sitting on the table.

"I like you too," said Etta.

"Josefina and Gar, why don't you join us at Hermitage Castle for a while?" asked Lord Dustin. "We've decided to leave first thing in the morning."

"Hermitage Castle?" asked Josefina.

"It's where the MacKeefes live. It's in the Lowlands on the border," explained Gar, ripping off a hunk of bread and offering it to her.

"I thought the MacKeefes were a Highland clan." Josefina took the bread from Gar.

"We are," answered Lark. "The MacKeefes have the castle and also a camp in the Highlands both."

"And the Horn and Hoof Tavern in Glasgow too?" asked Josefina, remembering what Lark had told her earlier.

"That too," said Martine. "Gar, why don't you and Josefina join us? And Etta, of course. I think it would be fun."

"I've got a job to do," said Gar. "I'm sorry, but I'm working."

As much as Josefina wanted to spend more time with these people, she knew Gar was right.

"I'm afraid we can't, but thank you for asking. We'll be at the trade fair here for a few more days and I'm not sure what's going to happen after that."

"I want to see where Florie lives," said Etta.

"I don't see why you can't go with them." Josefina looked over at Martine. "Would you take Etta with you to Hermitage Castle?"

"Where does Etta live?" asked Dustin.

"She doesna have parents. She's an orphan, just like the cat," said little Florie.

Suddenly Josefina felt bad. "Etta will be living with me from now on," she announced.

"I will?" asked Etta, her smile returning to her face. "And Banshee too?"

"Yes, Banshee too," she told the girl, feeling as if she'd made the right decision. "I don't have any children of my own. So, Etta, I'd be happy if you were my daughter from now on."

"Truly?" The girl looked choked up by the thought.

"Josefina, what are you saying?" asked Gar in a soft voice. "Mayhap you should think this over better first."

"Why?" she asked him, wondering why it would even matter to him. "I have no one. You will be marrying a noble-woman soon and having a family of your own. I may never remarry or have the chance to birth children. Nay, I've decided. Etta, you will be part of my family from now on."

"Thank you!" shrieked Etta, bounding out of her chair

and running over and throwing her arms around Josefina. "I would love to have you as my new mother. And I'd love for Gar to be my new father."

"Huh?" Gar was lifting a wooden cup for a drink and almost spilled it. "Nay." He shook his head. "I can't be your father."

"Why not?" asked the girl.

"He's going to marry a noblewoman, not me," said Josefina, hearing her voice crack as she said it.

"Oh," said Etta, going back to sit down by Florie.

"It's gettin' late. Time for bed, Florie," said her mother.

"Gar, you get the floor in our room," said Robin. "I'm sleeping on a pallet tonight."

"You can do what you want. I'll be sleeping on the ship to keep an eye on things," announced Gar.

"You will?" Josefina sounded disappointed. She really wanted him to stay at the inn with the rest of them.

"I got a bad feeling from Harry. I don't want him out of my sight."

"I think I should stay on the ship as well to watch the crew," said Josefina, not brave enough to look at the others when she said it. Especially not Martine and Robin.

"You do?" Gar raised one eyebrow and got that sexy look back in his eyes again.

"Etta, since you're leaving in the morning with the others for Hermitage Castle, you should stay here at the inn tonight," Josefina told the girl.

"Yay," said Florie, seeming happier with the decision than Etta.

"Will I see you again, Josefina?" asked Etta, looking suddenly frightened she'd be abandoned.

"I told you, you'll be my daughter from now on." Josefina put her hand atop the girl's. "I will see you as soon as my work is done and you'll have a new home. I promise."

"Thank you," said Etta, hugging her cat.

"Let's get going," Gar said, putting his arm around Josefina's waist, and speaking into her ear.

"It was so nice meeting all of you. I hope to see you again soon." Josefina, stood up to go.

"Wait," said Lark, hurrying over and handing a cloth bag to Josefina.

"What is this?" she asked.

"It's somethin' to get things goin'," she whispered.

Josefina knew exactly what she meant when she opened the bag and saw a bottle of Mountain Magic within. Yes, she might need a swig or two of this to relax her because she was sure this was the night that she was finally going to make love with Gar.

CHAPTER 15

"Cup will bring the last shuttle boat with the rest of the things to the ship as soon as they pack up," said Josefina, taking Gar's hand as he helped her step into the small boat being rowed by Harry.

"I still don't see why we can't leave for Denmark," complained Harry. "The trade we have set up will bring in some well-needed money."

"Donald left me with sufficient funds, so I'm not worried," said Josefina, taking a seat across from Harry while Gar sat on the other side at the bow of the small boat. "Besides, I pay you and the crew well."

"It's a shame to let an opportunity like this go," said Harry, starting to row, not wanting to give it up.

"I told you, it's going to storm," said Gar. "It would be too dangerous and I won't risk the ship or our lives and the lives of the crew. Now, not another word about it."

"Aye, Cap'n," mumbled Harry with a dissatisfied look upon his face.

Once they were back on the ship, Josefina instructed them to put their cargo back in the hold so the rain wouldn't ruin it.

"This is too much work," complained Wilkens. "We can at least leave the fruits and vegetables out. A little rain won't hurt them." He looked up at the sky. "Honestly, none of us thinks it is going to rain."

"I've been sailing my entire life and can tell by the smell of the air. Believe me, there is a bad storm approaching even if none of you believe it. Do as Josefina says," warned Gar, putting his arm around her.

"T-Bald, please watch for Cup with the last shuttle boat of goods," said Josefina. "I want to make sure he gets back on board before the rain starts."

"Aye, Josefina," answered T-Bald. "So, what are the plans for the rest of the trip?"

"We'll stay here in Dunbar for a few days before heading back to either Scarborough or Hythe."

"That's too long," said Harry. "We need to leave by tomorrow morning in order to make it to Denmark in time."

"Let it go," said Gar in a deep warning voice. "We're not continuing the trip."

"That's right," agreed Josefina. "Now please, stop asking."

Hothead Harry stomped away, throwing things around as usual. Two-Spit hurried after him.

"T-Bald, watch over things. I'm getting some sleep," said Gar, starting for the cabin with Josefina right behind him.

"Aye, Cap'n," said T-Bald, heading up to the sterncastle for the night.

They entered the cabin and Gar lit a candle, placing it on

the table for light. Josefina closed the door behind them, feeling nervous of what might happen this night, but anxious at the same time.

"Lock the door," he told her.

"What?" Her brows raised.

"There is a key in the lock. I never use it, but tonight, I don't want to be disturbed."

"Oh. All right." She turned the key in the lock, hearing it click, causing her heart to race. Was he wanting this because he planned on having some intimate time with her?

"It's been a long day," said Gar, removing his weapon belt. "I suggest we both get some sleep You take the pallet behind the curtain." He started to remove his tunic next.

"I'm not tired," she said. "I thought mayhap we could talk?"

He lowered his arms, his tunic falling back in place.

"Talk? About what?"

"I don't know," she said, removing the bag from her shoulder that held the bottle of Mountain Magic that Lark gave her. It clunked against the wood of the table. "Anything you want to talk about is fine."

"What have you got in the bag?" He dipped his hand inside and pulled out the bottle, making a deep noise in his throat that sounded like a cross between pleasure and dread. "Where did you get this?" He uncorked the bottle and took a sniff.

"It was the bottle of whisky from earlier. Lark gave it to me. Her great-grandfather makes the whisky, you know."

"Mountain Magic," he said, staring at the bottle as if he really wanted a swig. "This is something not to be messed with and only for serious drinkers."

"I guess the Highlanders drink it all the time," she told him. "Have some more. It will help you relax."

"It made me so tired earlier that I wasn't even able to help you at the fair. I don't know." He seemed to think about it but shook his head and put the cork back into the neck of the bottle. "Nay," he said, sinking down atop a barrel that served as a chair. "If I drink that, it'll only make me want to kiss you even more. I'm afraid I won't be able to control myself."

Josefina's heart lodged in her throat. It was exactly what she wanted him to do— to kiss her. She wanted to kiss him in return. But she wouldn't trick him into doing so by offering him more whisky.

"I understand," she said, reaching out and running her hand gently down the bottle. "As much as I want you to kiss me right now, I want it to be because you want to, and not for any other reason. Oh, well, good night." She turned to go, but he reached out and grabbed her arm. Slowly, she turned to face him.

"I want it more than anything right now. You've got to believe me." She saw the longing in his eyes and knew he spoke the truth.

"So do I, Gar." She blinked away the tears filling her eyes.

"I don't want to hurt you, Josefina. I don't mean physically. I mean—"

"I know what you mean. But it's my choice how I feel. Don't think you can ever control that."

"I'm going to marry a noblewoman. Even if we are intimate, it won't change that."

"For heaven's sake, I'm not asking you to marry me, Gar. I've already been married and I don't think it is for me. All I wanted is to feel loved for once in my life, but I guess it was silly of me to think it would be with you." She pulled out of his grip and continued walking toward the hanging curtain. She heard him get up and stopped when she felt his hands on the back of her shoulders.

"Turn around, Josefina. Turn around so I can kiss you the way you deserve to be kissed."

She took a deep breath, still blinking away her tears, slowly turning to face him. His hands cradled her face as he stared deeply into her eyes.

"I have never met anyone like you, sweetheart. You are a strong woman who fears nothing. You wear your heart on your sleeve and have said things to me that most people think but would never say aloud. Part of you calls to something deep within me and it is driving me mad. I can no longer ignore it."

"You are a good man," she said in a breathy whisper. "I know you have love in your heart but I think you are afraid to show it. You are scared of what others might think of you. You are always determined to do the right thing. But what is the right thing for you, Gar? That is a decision that no one can make for you. You know in your heart what you want, so do what makes you feel good about yourself, not what you think you are expected to do."

"I'm not afraid of anything," he told her, drinking her in with his intense eyes, heating up the area between them.

"Except giving your heart to a woman who isn't of your same status," she said, hitting the mark and making him shake his head.

"Mayhap you are right, but no more." He leaned over and kissed her gently at first. The desire inside her grew. She reached out for him and when he broke the connection, she pulled him toward her and kissed him hard and long, never wanting him to forget her.

"I see you are a woman who knows what she wants."

"I am," she admitted. "Are you going to deny me my wants and needs?"

"Who am I to keep you from being happy or feeling loved?" He scooped her up in his arms, causing her to gasp aloud.

"Gar," she said, wetting her lips with her tongue. "What are you doing?"

"Taking you to bed," he said, kissing her once again.

"My bed or... or yours?"

"Our bed," he told her, making the decision of their intimacy final. She didn't stop him, because she wanted this as much as he did.

Sitting her gently on the bed, he stepped back and removed first his boots and then his tunic.

Her gaze fastened on his chest and he noticed.

"You want to touch it, don't you?"

"Ever so much," she admitted, reaching out one hand but stopping and pulling back.

"Don't stop yourself." He took her hand in his, kissing it gently and then placing it against his broad chest. She ran both her hands down his chest, then back up, fanning out her fingers and even squeezing his biceps. He purposely clenched, making them rock-hard, making her giggle.

"You are so hard," she said, loving the feel of his physique.

"You have no idea." He nodded downward and when she looked, she saw his erection pressing against his breeches.

"If I don't remove my braies right now, I'm afraid they are going to split open."

He started to reach for the tie at his waist, but she stopped him.

"Let me," she said, her fingers trembling as she untied the knot and slowly pulled his trews lower. Since he was standing and she was sitting, when his erection was released it sprung forward, nearly hitting her in the face. "Oh!" she cried.

"Don't open your mouth like that unless you plan to use it."

She knew what he meant. He wanted her to taste him. It was something Donald used to make her do. She never wanted to do it with him, but with Gar, it was different. She couldn't stop looking at his manhood, and gently reached out to touch him. He inhaled deeply when her fingers touched his hardened form.

"You are beautiful and big," she told him, never seeing such a size in her life.

"Oh, Josefina, you make me tremble with excitement with just your touch. You don't know what you're doing to me."

"I think I know," she said, looking up at him as she leaned forward and opened her mouth. She took him in, using her lips and tongue to savor his essence, never wanting to forget it.

He moaned with desire, his hands gripping her shoulders as she pleasured him with just her mouth. "Stop," he begged her, breathing heavily. "God's eyes, stop already." She pulled back, confused.

"Don't you like this?" she asked him. "I thought men normally did."

"Oh, I like it, you little vixen. Too much, if you must know. But when I find my release I want it to be when I sink into the warm depths between your thighs, not in your mouth."

His words excited her like she'd never been before. Just the thought of Gar sliding his manhood into her made her not want to wait another minute.

"Take me," she whispered. "I want this more than anything. Please, do not deny me this one request."

"I could never deny you, my sweet, sweet, Josefina." He leaned toward her, kissing her on the mouth once again. His hands slid down her shoulders, then around to squeeze her breasts.

With her breathing labored, she could barely speak. "I am so hot. I need to remove my gown."

She reached for the ties on the bodice, but his hands got there first. He quickly pulled down her bodice, but she wore a shift underneath. To her surprise, he grabbed the front of her shift and ripped it right open. The cool air wafted against her bare skin. His action and the sound of the ripping cloth oddly excited her even more. The anticipation was driving her crazy.

Then his mouth was on her neck, nibbling and kissing. Her head fell back as he started licking her skin, fondling her breasts and playing with her nipples at the same time.

"Ooooh, Gar, I feel something I've never felt before."

"I promise you, by the end of the night, you will have experienced many new feelings." His mouth covered one breast and he sucked her hard, using his tongue to bring her nipple to a peak. At the same time, he laid her back on the pillow, sliding his hands under her gown, pulling down her hose and throwing them to the floor. Next, he slipped her gown up over her head and threw that to the floor as well. It left her totally naked and exposed. He was naked as well.

"What kind of experiences do you mean?" she asked.

"Well," he said, running his hands up the inside of her thighs, gently pushing her legs apart. "You pleasured me, and I think it is only fair that I pleasure you in the same way. Is that new to you?"

"The same way?" she asked, realizing he meant what she'd done with her mouth. "Oh, no. I don't think so. I've never had that done to me but I don't think I would like it."

"Mayhap you should give it a chance before you decide if you like it or not." He crawled up onto the bed, spreading her legs and lowering his head between her thighs. He lifted her off the bed, wrapping her legs around his shoulders and pleasured her with his mouth and tongue making her feel things she'd never felt before.

Moaning aloud with each flick of his tongue, she gripped his hair tightly, closing her eyes and releasing all her worries. And just when she felt as if she was about to reach her peak, he stopped and set her back down on the bed.

"Gar, what are you doing?" Her eyes sprang open. "Please, I am so close to release. Do not stop now." This made her panic. If he walked away from her now, she was sure she would die.

"I want us both to go over that precipice at the same time." He positioned himself and leaned over to kiss her, slipping his manhood between her thighs, making her squirm in dire anticipation.

"Oh, that feels so good," she said, her chest rising and falling since she couldn't seem to get enough air.

"Let me know if I'm hurting you and I'll stop."

"You stop and I'll be the one hurting you," she warned him, making them both laugh aloud. They found their rhythm and did the dance of love. She wrapped her legs around his waist as he slid in and out, bringing her higher and closer to ecstasy. Josefina couldn't help herself. It felt so good that when she reached her peak, she cried out loudly, not caring who might hear her.

He made grunts and groans of his own, sounding like a bear as he found his release as well. Then he fell to the bed next to her, pulling her atop his body, wrapping his arms around her protectively as they both lay there breathing hard, not even saying a word.

He smoothed down her hair, constantly giving her kisses atop her head. For such a gruff man when it came to the crew, he was so gentle and caring in private.

"You are like a lion when you are on deck or sailing the ship," she told him. "But like a lamb when it comes to intimacy. I like that."

"A lamb?" He pulled back and made a face. "You're saying that about my love-making?"

"Oh, nay. I didn't mean that," she said with a smile, realizing she might have offended his masculinity. "That, my lord, is much like a wildcat and I liked every minute of it."

"Gar," he told her.

"What?" She raised her head off his chest and looked at him curiously, not knowing what he meant.

"You called me, my lord. Just call me Gar when we are naked and wrapped in each other's arms."

"Oh, I see." Smiling, she lowered her head atop his chest again. "Mayhap I'll call you Edgar. After all, that is your full name, isn't it?" She heard the beating of his heart pick up again when she said that. He remained silent and didn't answer.

"Gar?" She sat up, noticing his face change. "Did I say something wrong?"

"Nay. Nay, of course not." He got up and walked over to the table.

"Where are you going?"

"I think I could use some of this, now." He held up the bottle of Mountain Magic and smiled.

"Of course," she said, patting the mattress. "Come back. Please. I was enjoying just lying here in your embrace."

"Then that is what we'll do for the rest of the night," he told her, crawling back into the small bed with her. It was designed for one, but just as cozy with two. "I hope I made you feel loved," he said, sitting with his back against the wall and pulling her closer. He pulled the blanket up around them and uncorked the bottle.

"Yes, you did." She reached out and pushed a strand of his long hair behind his ear. "Thank you, for that," she told him. "That is the very first time I've ever— I mean, the first time I've felt so loved."

"That was your first time finding release with a man, wasn't it?" he asked, knowing just what she'd meant. He took a swig of whisky and swallowed.

"Well, what if it was?" she asked. "Would that make you think less of me?" She grabbed the bottle from him and took a sip, closing her eyes when she swallowed the potent golden liquid.

"On the contrary, I feel good that I made you feel a way that no man has ever done before."

His sense of self-pride was showing, but she found it adorable and didn't even try to tell him she didn't need a man to feel that way, but it was much more fun to share it with someone.

"Yes, Edgar, you have a talent in bed that I'm sure women talk about all the time."

His smile faded and he took another swig of whisky.

"I'm sorry, I didn't mean to make you sound like a male whore. I just figured you've been with and satisfied many women, that's all."

That returned the smile to his face. "I can't deny that, and it doesn't bother me that you said it."

When he told her, she realized that what must be upsetting him was when she called him Edgar.

"Your father's name was Edgar, was it not?"

"Yes." He looked down at the bottle and ran his fingertip around the rim. "My mother named me after him, but, of course, I never knew him."

"That must have been hard. I mean, growing up without a father."

"Oh, I had a father. My uncle Garrett claimed me as his son when he married my mother."

"I see. So, what is it that upsets you when I use your full name, Edgar."

She didn't think he was going to tell her. But with another few swigs of the whisky he opened up to her.

"It's just that, I've only been called Edgar by my mother, and only when I was young."

"Oh, you mean everyone started calling you Gar?"

"My uncle started that, feeding his need of importance by saying it was like his name of Garrett. It bothered him too much to know that it was the pirates who killed his brother. He also thought my mother used my father, but she claims they really felt something for each other although I don't know nor do I care if it was true."

"Do you prefer to be called Edgar?"

"I've grown used to the name, Gar. I think it fits me better."

"Then I shall call you Gar. I'm sorry, I didn't mean to upset you."

He took another drink of whisky before answering. "I often think of how much my father suffered at the hands of the pirates. His death must have been awful."

"So, your mother had something to do with his death?"

"Nay. She didn't want him to die, but it was her father, the pirate, Captain Powell ap Llyr who killed him. That is why I don't like being called a pirate. I'm nothing like him and neither will I ever be."

"Of course, not." She rubbed her hand up and down his arm. "Wait a minute. I thought your mother was a noble."

"She was, but didn't know it. She was raised as a pirate, and acted like one. But when she married my uncle, she changed. She is a wonderful woman."

"I am sure she is," said Josefina. "I would like to meet her, as well as your uncle someday."

"I would like that too, but I am not sure that will ever happen."

She knew he was thinking about his orders from the king again. That was the last thing she wanted right now.

Kissing him gently on the mouth, she did what she could to make him feel relaxed and carefree.

"Tonight, we will only think of happy things," she told him.

"Like what?" he asked.

"Well, like the fact we've had a wonderful night together. And that it doesn't have to end." She grabbed the bottle and took another drink and handed it back to him.

"Oh, I guess it doesn't." He did the same.

"Let's think of nothing that upsets us tonight." She ran a lazy finger over his chest, circling his nipple, making it erect. That made her giggle. Then she put her mouth over it, the way he did to her.

"Keep that up and we're going to be experiencing round two," he told her in a deep voice, looking and sounding so sexy.

"Only two rounds?" she asked playfully, letting her hand slip down his chest and below his waist.

"I don't know what kind of beast you think I am to be able to do it again so quickly," he said.

"Take your time. We have all night."

"You surely are a true vixen," he said, rubbing his hand down her back.

"And you are a lamb in a wolf's clothing."

"Stop calling me a lamb. I'll show you I'm more of a lion or wolf than a lamb."

"That is exactly what I was hoping for," she said, taking another sip of Mountain Magic and handing him the bottle. This was going to be one night that she was never going to forget!

CHAPTER 16

Gar was in the middle of a nightmare where he was on a pirate ship and a battle broke out. He could hear the sound of the anchor chain as well as the sails whipping in the wind. In the dream, he was unable to move. A storm moved in with lightning flashing across the sky and thunder booming overhead. Rain pelted down around him as the ship went into a whirlpool of water, sucking them down to the bottom of the sea. As the ship disappeared under the waves, he could hear the continuous pounding in his ears that a man underwater experiences before losing his life to the violent sea.

"Nay!" He sprang up in bed to a sitting position, gasping for breath. His heart beat so rapidly, he thought it would burst out of his chest. He looked down to see Josefina sleeping next to him. She stirred and made a soft cooing noise. This should have settled him, but for some reason he had the feeling that something was terribly wrong.

"Cap'n, wake up," came a muffled voice from the other

side of the door. The pounding continued as someone knocked.

"What the hell." Gar jumped out of bed, losing his balance as he tried to don his trews in the dark. The ship was rolling back and forth. This shouldn't be so violent since they were anchored and not moving. Something wasn't right.

"Gar? What's happening?" came Josefina's sleepy voice from the bed. After finishing off the bottle of Mountain Magic between them last night, Gar wasn't feeling all that well. He was surprised he was even conscious since that strong whisky had ill effects on a man.

"Cap'n, are you in there?" He now recognized Cup's voice from the other side of the door.

"Why is the ship rocking so much?" Josefina sat up and tried to get out of bed but fell back down.

"I have a bad feeling about this." After donning his boots, he ripped open the hanging blanket that served as a curtain. Through the window on the other side he could see a bad storm raging. "We're in the middle of a storm. Get dressed, quickly." Gar threw Josefina's gown to her. Then he grabbed his tunic and ran to the window as he pulled it over his head. "Bid the devil, my nightmare has come true."

"What does that mean?" Josefina sat on the bed, pulling her gown over her head.

"Cap'n, come quickly. You're needed."

"Isn't that Cup's voice? What is going on?" she asked him.

"We're no longer anchored," he told her, donning his weapon belt. "We're in the midst of a bad storm and out at sea. Damn it, why didn't I hear the anchor chain or feel the movement of the ship?"

"Oh, I don't feel so well." Josefina got up and grabbed a bucket in the corner and threw up.

Gar turned the key and yanked open the door. A soaking wet Cup fell up against him.

"Captain, there's a bad storm and we need you. Hothead Harry can't control the ship."

"Harry is behind this? Dammit, I'll grind him under my heel after lopping off his head."

He heard Josefina vomiting again and turned, not wanting to leave her but having no choice. "Will you be all right?" he asked her.

"Yes," she said with a nod, her face taking on a tinge of green. "I think I drank too much Mountain Magic. And with the ship lulling back and forth, it is upsetting my stomach even more.

"Get back in bed and stay there," he commanded. "Harry's taken over the ship and we're in the middle of a bad storm."

"All right," she said, holding on to things, making her way back to the bed.

"No matter what happens, do not come out onto the deck. Do you understand me?" he asked. "I don't have time to protect you and save the ship as well."

"I understand." She held the bucket in front of her, looking as if she were going to be sick again.

"Where the hell is T-Bald?" Gar asked the boy. "I told him to guard the ship."

"He was at the stern when I boarded the ship last night," Cup told him. "But Harry decided to take us to Denmark. He knocked out T-Bald and tied him up. He threatened to kill the rest of us if we went against his wishes."

"Damn it, why didn't you wake me up earlier?" Gar ran out onto the deck, almost falling since the rain was coming down so hard and the deck was slick. Plus, the ship was rocking so badly that it was impossible to walk a straight line.

"I wanted to, but couldn't," said the boy. "Harry had Two-Spit Sam guarding your door and he wouldn't let anyone near the cabin. When I finally got past him, the door was locked. That is why I was knocking."

"Why didn't I trust my instincts?" Gar found T-Bald on the floor tied up right at the foot of the steps leading to the helm. Ripping his dagger out of his waistbelt, Gar cut him free and removed his gag.

"I'm sorry, Captain. Harry took me by surprise," apologized the old man.

"Get up," growled Gar, looking around. The crew was frantic, trying to ride out the storm. Harry was at the helm, doing nothing productive to steer the ship out of this mess. "Follow me," he told T-Bald, darting up the steps, grabbing Harry and punching him hard. Harry fell to the floor while T-Bald grabbed the wheel to steer the ship. "I'll kill you, you rotten piece of dung. Why did you take the ship out when I told you a storm was approaching?"

"It didn't look like rain." Harry got up with his mouth bleeding. "Besides, you have no right to tell us not to go to Denmark. I had to get us there. It's what Donald would have wanted."

"Donald probably didn't even have a trade, but was just

meeting one of his favorite whores." He hit the man again, sending him sprawling against the side wall.

"Captain, I'm having trouble," called out T-Bald from the helm. "The wind is too strong. I can't turn the tiller."

"Dammit," Gar swore again, running to help T-Bald. The wheel was two wheels together with a post in between. A rope wrapped around it and went through the floor attached to the tiller in the bowels of the ship. When the wheel was turned, it pulled the rope one way or another, hence moving the tiller. The tiller swung around and moved the rudder. This is what steered the ship.

It took the strength of the two of them together to pull the wheel, but the storm raging around them was only making things worse.

"Shorten the sails. Reef the main sail. Quickly! This wind is trying to take us all straight to hell," shouted Gar.

"We're working on it, Cap'n," called out Solobow.

Lightning continued to slash across the sky and thunder boomed loudly. The waves were so high that they splashed over the sidewalls and onto the deck almost washing the crew overboard.

"Captain, I'm sorry," said Harry, wiping blood from his face. "I didn't mean for this to happen."

"It's a little too late for that now," yelled Gar. "We'll be lucky to ride out the storm. But by the way it is looking, luck isn't on our side. Get over there and help the crew with the sails," he told him.

"Aye, Cap'n." Harry took a few steps but turned around before descending the stairs. "I'm sorry about that, T-Bald, but I knew you would side with the captain and I had to stop you."

"Go!" shouted Gar, sick of Harry's voice and his lame apologies that meant nothing anymore since it was looking like the ship might go down in the storm and they would all die.

Josefina jumped when the door to the cabin flew open and banged against the wall. Gar must not have closed it securely. With the rocking of the ship, it opened on its own.

"Help! Help me," she thought she heard a small voice on the wind. It sounded like that of a girl. Josefina put down the bucket and held on to whatever she could, making her way to the open door. Once there, she looked out at the storm. The sky was black and lightning lit up the area showing her the damage already on the ship. The waves were so high they were washing things right over the side of the ship. It was the most frightening thing she'd ever seen.

"Secure the rigging! Batten down the hatches, damn it," shouted Gar. "We're losing everything and soon it will be men as well."

The waves kept washing over the sidewall and the crew had trouble even standing. They looked frantic as they tried to continue to carry out the orders, some of them hanging by their knees from the lines. She left the cabin and looked back at the sterncastle to see Gar and T-Bald trying to steer the ship through the raging storm.

Josefina suddenly remembered her promise to stay in the cabin. She was about to go back inside when she heard the screech of an animal. She looked up and saw something falling from the mast. When she raised her arms to block herself from getting hit, a cat fell into her arms and against her chest. Frightened out of her mind, she pushed it away and looked down to the deck to see a wet spotted cat looking up at her with large, scared green eyes.

"Banshee?" she asked in surprise. "What are you doing here? I thought you were with Etta. She bent down and scooped up the cat before it was washed overboard.

"Help," came that same little voice on the wind once again. When she looked upward and shaded her eyes from the rain, she saw someone up in the ratlines, hanging on for dear life in the storm.

"Who is that?" she said to herself, cradling the scared cat against her. The person seemed much too small to be one of the men of the crew.

"It's Etta." Cup swung down on a line, dropping next to her.

"Etta? Nay, she went to Hermitage Castle with Lady Martine. Didn't she?" Josefina looked down to the cat in her arms, knowing that Etta would never leave her new pet behind.

"No, she didn't," said Cup. "I brought her and the cat back in the shuttle boat with me last night."

"You did? Why?"

"She told me you said she could stay on the ship with you."

"No, I didn't. And why didn't she tell me she was here?"

"She probably didn't want to get in trouble for disobeying your orders," said Cup. "I guess that's why I saw her climbing up to the lookout basket last night to sleep there."

"Oh, poor Etta. This is terrible. I've got to help her." The ship rolled again and Cup held on to her when she almost fell. "Cup, take Banshee and lock her inside the cabin. Bring back my cloak. Hurry."

Cup did as told, returning with her cloak and helping her to don it.

"I'd climb up there to help her, but I'm still feeling ill and queasy." She was sure she'd vomit again any minute.

"Nay, you can't go up there. It's too dangerous in the storm."

"What about you?" she asked. "Can you climb up and help her down?"

"Cup! Get over here now," shouted Crusty Rusty. "We need you to help batten down the hatches. Plus, the water is getting into the hold."

"Oh, nay," she said. "It'll ruin my fine silks. Go, help them," she told the boy. "I'll tell Gar about Etta."

The boy ran off to join the rest of the crew. Holding on to whatever she could, Josefina made her way to the foot of the stairs leading up to the sterncastle. "Gar!" she shouted, trying to be heard above the raging wind. She clung to the railing, almost losing her footing once again. "Gar, I need you."

Gar had enough trouble on his hands, but when he saw Josefina at the foot of the stairs, he groaned. "I thought I told you to stay in the cabin," he yelled.

"It's Etta," she said.

"What?"

"Etta is up there." She pointed up to the center mast.

Gar's attention was drawn to someone hanging on to the lines. He thought at first it was one of the crew, but then he realized just what Josefina said. That troublesome girl was up in the lines in the storm.

"God's eyes, nay," he said, turning to T-Bald. "Keep her steady and head her away from the storm," he told him. "It's our only hope not to capsize. We've got to ride out this storm. I've got a girl to save. Again."

"Aye, Cap'n."

Gar bolted down the stairs, taking ahold of Josefina's arm. "What the hell is going on?"

"Etta is up in the lines," she told him. "I'm afraid she's going to fall. She went up there with her cat last night, but the cat is in the cabin now."

"I thought she was with Martine and Robin."

"So did I. The girl seems to have trouble listening."

"You are going back to the cabin before I even attempt to rescue her," commanded Gar, thinking only of Josefina's safety.

"Nay. I am Etta's mother now, and I will not abandon her."

"Josefina, do you trust me?" he asked, looking deeply into her eyes. The storm continued and the men shouted, all of them trying to keep the ship from going down.

"Of course, I do," she told him.

"Then go to the cabin and lock yourself inside. I don't want you getting swept overboard. I have my hands full and I cannot watch after you at the same time as trying to help a daft girl, command a rebellious crew, and save the ship of my dreams."

"I'll go, Gar. And I know you'll save Etta." She reached up

and kissed him, then looked as if she were going to puke again. "Please be careful."

"You don't have to tell me that. Now go!"

He waited until he saw Josefina go into the cabin and close the door. Then he took hold of the lines and started to climb.

"Captain, what are you doing?" called out Solobow. "We've got the sails secure and there is no reason to risk your life up there."

"Oh, yes there is," he said, feeling like he was living his nightmare all over again. The only thing missing was pirates. "Etta, hold on. I'm coming," he called to the frightened girl.

The wind whipped around him, almost pushing him from the lines. When he looked up again, he heard Etta scream. Her fingers slipped from the ropes and she dangled from the ratlines, only being held up by her legs.

"God's teeth, I knew females aboard were only going to cause trouble." He made it to her, stretching out his arm, but she was just out of reach. "Etta, reach out and take my hand," he told the girl.

"I'm too scared. I'm falling. And Banshee fell and is probably dead."

"Nay. Banshee is safe in the cabin with Josefina. Just where you should be."

Lighting struck the top of the mast, catching the lookout basket on fire.

"Aaaaaah," screamed the girl.

Gar hoped the heavy rain would put out the fire before it spread. With the sails lowered, they wouldn't catch fire. He climbed a little higher, holding on by only his legs, reaching out and grabbing the girl just as her legs gave way and she fell. He pulled her to his chest, clinging to the lines with his free hand.

"You're safe now, Etta," he told the girl who buried her face against his chest, bawling. Her little body shook from the cold and from fear. "I've got you and you don't need to worry. I won't let you fall."

"Thank you, Father," she said, making him feel choked with emotion. He'd never been called Father before. Although it was odd, he rather liked it. The only thing was, he didn't have the heart to tell the girl he couldn't be her father, because there was no way in hell he could marry Josefina. Even after the wonderful, intimate night he'd spent with Josefina in his bed, he still needed to follow the king's orders. He needed to marry a noblewoman even though he'd fallen in love with a woman he could never have.

CHAPTER 17

By the time Gar got things under control and the storm stopped, it was already daybreak. The sun on the horizon lit up the fog hanging low over the water, making it hard to see far at all. Gar was so tired, he thought he'd fall over. Still, he needed to get back to the coast. He'd turned the ship around and now T-Bald was at the helm.

While he and Josefina slept, Hothead Harry had managed to take the ship far from the coast. They were still closer to Scotland than they were to Denmark, and all he wanted to do was to get the girls safely on shore. Never had he had such trouble while sailing as he had this time. This was the ship of his dreams, but those dreams had turned to nightmares lately. He glanced up at the lookout basket that had been struck by lightning and caught fire. It still smoldered, but he needed to know the extent of the damage and that the fire was totally extinguished before he gave the command to raise the sails.

"Did anyone go up to the lookout to check on the damage?"

"Nay, Cap'n," one of the men called out.

"Did you want me to go?" It was Cup, always wanting to help. But he was young and Gar wasn't sure he had the experience it took to do the jobs of the rest of the crew. He didn't want to risk it, and didn't see Rusty or Solobow anywhere.

"Nay. I'll go," said Gar. "You go to the cabin and check on the girls. Tell Josefina, I'll be there soon."

"Aye, aye, Cap'n." Cup hurried off to carry out his orders.

One last time, Gar took hold of the ratlines and climbed to the basket where he and Josefina had shared a few kisses. He smiled, thinking of the night they'd spent together. His heart ached to know he'd probably led her on. The last thing he wanted to do was to hurt her.

He got up to the basket and stepped inside, stomping out a stray flame. One side was scorched, but it was nothing that couldn't easily be fixed. He checked the masts and lines and couldn't see any real damage.

"All's clear. Hoist the sails, Solobow."

"Aye, Cap'n," came the man's reply from the deck.

Gar was about to descend, when something caught his attention. Above the low floating fog in the distance, he swore he saw the mast of a ship. Looking more carefully, he could just make out what he was seeing.

"God's eyes, nay," he said, turning and shouting to the crew below. "Black sails," he called out.

"What did you say?" Rusty looked up, shouting back to him.

"Pirates! Full speed ahead and don't slow down until I

give the command." Gar made his way down the lines faster than he ever had in his life. "Nay, stay straight," he called out, realizing the ship was turning to the port, which was the direction of the pirate ship.

"Captain, we've got a problem," called out T-Bald from the helm.

"What now?" Gar bolted up the steps to the sterncastle to find T-Bald shaking his hairless head. "What's the matter?"

"The storm was too much for her," said T-Bald, speaking about the ship. "The tiller rope has snapped."

"Nay!" screamed Gar, not wanting to hear any more bad news. "Without being able to move the rudder, we're dead in the water," he said. "And now, we've got a pirate ship approaching."

"Did you say pirate ship?" Josefina appeared at the top of the steps with Etta right behind her. Etta cradled her cat in her arms.

"Bid the devil, Josefina, not now. Take the girl back to the cabin. This is no place for either of you."

"Don't forget, this is my ship." Josefina's hands went to her hips. "Now, tell me everything. I need to know what is going on."

Gar took a deep breath and slowly released it, not wanting to explode with anger. "Well, my dear, besides the storm almost capsizing us, now the tiller rope is broken."

"Broken? Well, can it be fixed?"

"You are the daughter of a shipwright. You tell me." It was a waste of time trying to explain this to a woman.

"Well," she said, putting her hand to her chin in thought. "If I remember correctly, my father said it could be fixed at sea if you attached chains directly to the tail end of the rudder and pulled on that to steer the ship.

Gar was actually impressed that she knew that, or even that she realized how the steering of a ship worked. "True," he said. "But that takes time. Time that we don't have because a Goddamned pirate ship is chasing us!" He shouted the last part, not able to control his temper any longer.

"There really is a pirate ship, then?" she asked. "Where?"

"There." He pointed and she squinted her eyes to see, and then her eyes opened wide.

"Oh, no! We're about to be attacked. What are we going to do?"

"If you'd give me a minute to think and if I could stop answering all your questions, I'd be happy to tell you."

"Mother, I'm scared," said Etta, still clinging to Banshee as well as Josefina's arm now.

"Captain, we can't outrun them with our situation," said T-Bald.

"And we're headed straight for them now," added Two-Spit, walking up the steps to join them.

"Then we'll have to go below deck and move the tiller by hand," said Gar.

"By hand? Is that possible?" asked Josefina.

"It's not easy, but at least it'll put us back on course. With the wind at our back, we might still have a chance to get away," Gar told her.

"I'll head the crew below deck to move the tiller," offered Hothead Harry, coming up behind Two-Spit. "I feel this is all my fault."

"Of course, it is," growled Gar. "But I don't want your

help. I want nothing from you, Harry, because I can no longer trust you. For all I know, you're one of the pirates and you were trying to lead us to them."

"Harry? Are you?" asked Josefina.

"Am I what?"

"You know what I mean. Are you a pirate?" asked Josefina.

"Nay. But mayhap our captain is the true pirate, wanting to go back to his old ways."

That did it. Gar snapped and pushed the others aside, grabbing Harry by his throat, wanting to strangle him right there.

"Gar, let him go," said Josefina. "If he said he's not a pirate, then I believe him."

"How can we ever believe a word he says?" asked Gar, still pressing his fingers into Harry's neck. Harry made choking noises and Gar didn't care if he killed him right now. Because of this fool man's actions, they might have all lost their lives in the storm. And even though they survived, with a broken tiller rope they were nothing but bait for hungry pirates. Gar couldn't even imagine what the pirates would do if they found Josefina or Etta. He would kill every pirate by his own hand before he ever let them harm the girls.

"Trust me, Gar. Let him go," pleaded Josefina.

Josefina's voice was uncannily calm. It helped Gar come back to his senses. He released Harry who fell backward, still coughing, having to be caught by Solobow coming up the steps.

"Captain, the crew is awaiting your orders," said Solobow.

"Of course." Gar took one more deep breath and released it. "Solobow, take a dozen men with you and be ready to hoist or lower the sails as needed. Harry, take another dozen men and go below deck and listen for T-Bald's commands on which way to move the tiller."

"Aye, Cap'n," both the men answered, hurrying down the steps.

"And Harry," he said, causing Harry and Two-Spit to stop and turn around. "Don't even think of deceiving me again, because next time Josefina might not be around to talk me out of breaking your damned neck."

Harry nodded as the men ran around to carry out Gar's orders.

"Do you want to take the helm?" asked T-Bald.

"Nay," said Gar. "With the broken rope, there is nothing we can do up here right now. I've got to get the rest of the men armed and ready to fight when the pirates board the ship."

"Are we going to die? Will the pirates kill us, Father?" cried Etta.

"Not if I can help it, and I'm not your father and will never be. Now go with Josefina down to the hold and hide there until I tell you it's safe to come out."

"Not in the cabin?" asked Josefina.

"Nay. It's the first place they'll look once they board."

"Won't they look in the hold for cargo to pilfer?" Josefina still seemed calm even though there was every reason not to be right now. The woman was truly amazing.

"I'm not planning on letting them get that far," answered Gar. "Now, go. And do what I say this time. I cannot have one more distraction."

"I understand," said Josefina, taking Etta's hand and leading the way down the steps. She stopped and looked back up at him.

"What is it?" he asked.

"In case I never have a chance again to tell you... I love you, Edgar Blackmore," said Josefina, hurrying away with the girl before he could even respond and tell her that he loved her as well.

Josefina pulled Etta into the cabin and closed the door. She'd rushed away from Gar, not wanting him to see the tears in her eyes. And while she'd admitted her feelings for him, she knew he didn't share them and left before he could remind her again that he was about to leave her and marry a noble-woman and they'd never see each other again.

"I thought Father said we were to hide in the hold," said Etta, putting down the cat. Banshee jumped up to the table, sniffing around for scraps of food.

"That is exactly where you're going to be." Josefina grabbed her cloth bag, handing it to Etta. "Put the cat inside and don't let her get away again. Do you want food? Are you hungry?"

"I know where to find food in the hold," said the girl, picking up the cat and putting her in the cloth bag.

"Yes, I suppose you do know how to survive since you've been on your own so long."

"Mother. Josefina, I have something I need to tell you."

"Not now. There will be plenty of time later."

"Nay. I have to say it now."

"All right. What?" Josefina crossed her arms over her chest.

"I lied to Lady Martine and Lady Lark. I told them that you said I could stay on the ship with you and Gar."

"I already figured," said Josefina. "Just like you lied about your age. Is there anything else you lied about?"

"Right before my mother died, she told me about this ship and that I should come here. It took me a year on my own to find it."

"Why would she do such a thing?"

"Because she said I have a brother."

"A brother? Who? What do you mean?"

"She said she couldn't raise both of us alone. Since my brother was five years older than me, she sent him off to work on the ship called the *Lady Josefina*."

"What? Really? So your brother is here on the ship now?"

"I don't know," said the girl, putting her hand inside the bag to pet the cat. I was only three when he left and I don't remember much about him. Only his name."

"And what is that?"

"His name is Cyprian."

Josefina gasped. "Cup," she said. "He's your brother?"

"He is?" Etta thought for a minute and narrowed her eyes. "He might be. Yes, I think he could be."

"Why didn't Cup know you? Or at least recognize you by your name?" asked Josefina.

"Well, I was very young and looked different when he knew me. Plus, everyone called me Wilmetta. It wasn't until I was older that I told Mother I'd rather be called Etta."

"So, Cup, or Cyprian was about eight when he started working for my husband," said Josefina. That was years before she was even married to Donald. Josefina had never thought to even ask Cup about his background. Now she felt bad.

"I want to see my brother," said Etta.

"Not now. You need to go hide in the hold like Gar said." Josefina hurried the girl to the door of the cabin.

"But he might get killed by the pirates. I want to talk to him."

"You can do that later. Now is not the time." Josefina pulled Etta out on the deck, almost having to drag her to the door of the hold. "Now stay quiet and keep Banshee from wandering off. We'll come down to get you when we're out of danger."

"You're not coming with me?"

"Nay."

"But where will you be?"

Josefina looked back to see Gar loading more weapons into his belt and handing out swords and daggers to the rest of the crew, giving them instructions for when the pirates boarded. Even though some of the men had gone down below deck to try to move the tiller by hand, they were still headed straight for the pirate ship. It floated through the fog, getting so close that she was able to see the black flags atop their masts. Terror filled her now, because this was real. Pirates were about to board their broken vessel, and hell if Josefina was going to hide while they took the life of the man she loved.

"I'm going to be fighting off pirates along with Gar," she told the girl.

"You're going to fight?"

"Why not?" asked Josefina.

"Then I'm going to fight too." Etta pulled out the dagger she'd stolen from the whore at the tavern and held it high in the air. Banshee stuck her head out of the bag and started mewing loudly.

"Nay, you're not." Josefina, helped her down the steps leading into the dark hold. "Now, keep that dagger for protection if the pirates come down here. But don't fight unless they try to hurt you. Keep hidden inside an empty apple barrel. You'll be safe there. Do you hear me?"

"I don't want to lose another mother and father and brother, or Banshee," said Etta looking so sad that it about broke Josefina's heart.

"You won't. Everything will be fine," she told the girl. "Trust me and just stay hidden." Josefina reached down and kissed the girl on the cheek, then turned and ran up the steps, closing the door to the hold behind her. "I hope I can keep my word," Josefina mumbled, seeing the pirate ship almost upon them now. They were so close that she could see the pirates holding up their swords. They had grappling hooks attached to ropes and long poles they would use for boarding. Gar was standing on the sterncastle looking out at the ship. He had a sword in one hand and an axe in the other.

"God, be with us," she prayed, running for the cabin to get the sword from under the floorboard in the cabin, a weapon that Donald had always kept there. With that, along with her eating knife, she'd be armed. Not that she knew how to even use a sword but still, she had to help Gar however she could. The last thing she ever wanted was to lose him.

CHAPTER 18

Gar stood atop the sterncastle of the ship with his weapons in hand, but feeling like his nightmare had come to life and it was all about to be over soon, one way or another. Even with the men below deck trying to move the tiller by hand, it was too late. They weren't going to be able to outrun the pirate ship. The pirates were about to board and all they could do was fight.

He prayed that he and the crew could at least keep the pirates away from the hold where Josefina and Etta were safe for now. But these men aboard the *Lady Josefina* were not trained in fighting like he was. Nay, they were only sailors. Most of them didn't have more than a dagger on them. Thankfully, the ship was stocked with weapons to use, meant for times like this if they had to fight at sea.

"Rusty, Two-Spit, are the men armed and ready?" shouted Gar.

"We are," Two-Spit called back. "But it looks like we're severely outnumbered."

Gar had noticed that too. They needed the help of every man there. Even the cabin boy held a weapon, ready to fight alongside the men.

"Cup, go below deck and tell Harry I need all the men up here armed with weapons right now. We have one chance at this, and it isn't looking promising."

"Aye, Cap'n," shouted Cup, running to get the rest of the crew.

Gar saw the pirates clearly aboard their ship now and it brought back memories of the pirates he once considered his family. When he was a boy, he felt safe and protected having pirates on his side. Now, he felt as vulnerable as a rabbit being chased by a lion.

"They're going to board," Gar shouted to his men. "Axemen, cut the grappling lines as soon as they hit our sidewall."

"Aye, aye, Cap'n," shouted his crew, raising their axes and moving closer to the sidewall.

"No pirate lives," he called out again. "Take down any of them that step aboard our ship."

"Cap'n, the crew isn't prepared for this," said T-Bald coming to his side with a sword in his hand. "They're not trained for war. This won't be a fair fight. The pirates will pick us off easily and take the ship and cargo."

"You're not telling me anything I don't already know." Gar would do his part to fight off the pirates and protect the girls, the crew, and also the ship. But he was just one man. This was going to be a bloody slaughter. He wished Robin was here with him right now. Then again, it would probably mean his death too, so mayhap it was better that he and Martine weren't present.

"Throw the grappling hooks!" yelled the pirate captain.

The sickening sound of clinking against their hull made Gar want to retch.

"Cut the lines!" shouted Gar, hoping they could hold the pirates off if they couldn't pull the *Lady Josefina* close enough to board.

A line of men with axes hurried forward, cutting the grappling lines with success. But then the pirates started swinging on ropes and dropping onto the deck of Gar's ship.

"Dammit, nay," he grunted, rushing forward to fight off the closest one. His sword clashed with the pirate's in a fierce battle.

"You'll never fight us all off," growled the pirate. "This ship is ours. Surrender."

"Never!" With a forceful thrust, Gar stabbed the pirate through the heart, pushing the man's body overboard.

T-Bald fought at his side as more and more pirates somehow managed to get aboard the ship. Several of the pirates had bows with flaming arrows that they shot through the air, taking down a half dozen of Gar's crew.

"Nay!" he screamed, barreling down the steps to help. "Put out the flames," he yelled to no one in particular, not wanting the ship to go up like a torch. Every man was occupied fighting and it would take too long to fetch pails of water. Gar yanked an arrow from a dead man, stomping out the flame. Seeing a pirate headed right for him, he fought like a madman, knowing he had to save Josefina and Etta. But how in God's name was he ever going to do that now?

Josefina emerged from the cabin with her weapons, barely able to even lift the heavy sword. As soon as she stepped out on deck, she froze. Pirates were boarding the ship and there were so many of them. Gar was at the front of the line fighting them off with the crew doing all they could to help. Her heart raced and fear engulfed her. There was also fire. At least half a dozen men lay dead and bleeding with flaming arrows sticking out of their chests.

"I've got to help," she said to herself, getting pushed aside by the men running from below deck to join the fight.

"Where do you think you're going?" asked Hothead Harry, carrying a large axe on a pole over his shoulder.

"I'm going to help fight off the pirates," she told him.

"Like hell you are," said Harry.

"Don't try to stop me, Harry. I have to help Gar. Besides, this is my ship and I won't surrender it to those blackhearts."

"All you're going to do is distract the captain and cause his death."

"Nay. I'm going to help. I want to help. I cannot hide away and do nothing."

"I've already done the captain wrong," said Harry. "He'll have my head if he knows I let you on the deck in the middle of an attack. Now get back into the cabin and stay there."

"I won't!"

"Oh, yes, you will." Harry grabbed her gruffly by the arm and dragged her to the cabin and opened the door. "And give me that before you hurt yourself." He pulled the sword away from her and headed to the door.

"You can't tell me what to do. I'm not staying in here

when Gar's life and the life of every man of my crew is in danger." She followed him to the door.

"I said stay!" He pushed her and she fell to the floor. He took the key out of the lock and looked back at her. "I'll lock you in if I have to."

"No. Please don't do that. Gar needs me."

"I'm wasting precious time." Harry left, closed the door and locked it from the other side.

"Nay!" she cried, running to the door and pulling on it, but it wouldn't budge. He'd locked her in and now there was nothing she could do but sit and listen to men being killed right outside her door. She dropped to her knees, blessing herself to pray. "Please watch over Gar," she whispered. "And Etta and Cup and Banshee and all the rest of the crew."

Feeling trapped, alone, and totally helpless, Josefina cried hard because she knew this would be the end of them all.

CHAPTER 19

"Harry, get over here," Gar shouted, seeing Harry emerge with the rest of the crew from below deck. "Our numbers are dropping fast."

"I've got you covered." Harry fought at Gar's side as pirate after pirate boarded their ship and there was nothing he could do to stop them. The wind picked up and the sky darkened once again. It looked to be another storm approaching. Just what they didn't need.

"I found Josefina with weapons, headed this way," said Harry, taking down a pirate.

"God's eyes, nay. Where is she? I told her to take Etta and hide in the hold."

"No worries, Cap'n. I locked her in the cabin. She won't be able to get out."

"Good," said Gar. That was until he heard Wilkens from across the deck.

"Fire! The main sail is on fire," called out Wilkens.

Things went from bad to worse as the strong winds spread the fire from the flaming arrows, catching the sail.

Gar spun around to look. The ship was going up like a torch. And Etta was hiding in the hold while Josefina had no chance of escaping the fire locked inside the cabin. "God's teeth, can this get any worse?"

"Captain, behind you!" shouted Harry.

Gar spun around to see a nasty pirate with his sword raised, lowering it right at him. Harry jumped in front of Gar, pushing him to the side. The pirate's blade stabbed Hothead Harry right through the heart. Harry clutched his chest and dropped his weapon. Blood spit out from his mouth as his knees buckled and he fell to the floor. In saving Gar's life, Harry sacrificed his own.

"You scurvy dog, you'll die for that!" Gar stabbed his blade into the pirate, pushing the dead man down and yanking his sword from his chest. "Harry, oh, Harry." Gar knelt down, seeing the man was too injured and already lost too much blood. He was nearly dead.

"I'm... sorry. About... everything, Cap'n," said Harry, his eyes looking up at Gar in fear. "I should have listened to you. I... was... wrong." Harry died with his eyes open. The man had brought Josefina to safety and saved Gar's life. Mayhap he wasn't as bad as Gar had thought, but there was no time for reflecting on the past and surely no time for regrets.

Gar stood up and looked around him, feeling numb. The ship of his dreams was going up in flames. The crew was being picked off quickly and more and more pirates were boarding the ship. They were all doomed. He had tried his best, but they were all going to die here today and the worst part was that Josefina and Etta would die as well. That is, if the pirates didn't take them back to their ship to use them as they pleased.

There was a flash of lightning and a loud crack.

"The mast is falling! Look out!" shouted Rusty.

As if being punished by God above, once again their ship was hit by lightning and this time the mast split and fell across the door to the hold.

"Etta," he said, thinking of the young orphan girl and her cat hiding in the hold. The girl who had called him Father was going to die. Gar never had a chance to be the father to her that she longed for after losing her own. Now, he regretted being so harsh and telling her he wasn't her father and that he was never going to be.

"Arrrgh!" yelled a pirate causing Gar to spin around, using one hand to throw his dagger and his other to fight with his sword. He managed to kill two of them, but luck wasn't on his side today when he realized at least a dozen more of his crew lay dead at his feet.

"I've got to get to Josefina and Etta," he said, trying to fight his way over to the cabin and the hold. However, even when he got there, he had no plan on how he'd help the girls because there was nowhere for them to go.

Josefina pounded on the door to the cabin and shouted, hearing a loud crash from the other side. "What is going on? Let me out. I want to help," she cried, her fist raw from pounding so hard against the wood. Then, to her surprise, she heard the key turn in the lock from the other side. She quickly drew her dagger as the door slowly opened. She prayed it wasn't a pirate on the other side. But her will to get out and not be locked in again was stronger than her fear of a pirate at the moment. Josefina yanked the door wide open, letting out a gasp of relief when she saw Etta standing there with Banshee in her arms.

"Etta! It's you, thank goodness." She pulled the girl to her in a hug. That's when she noticed the broken, burning mast blocking the door to the hold. "You could have been trapped down there," she whispered.

"I came to find you. I was scared."

"I'm glad you did."

"Josefina! Etta! I'm coming to save you."

She looked up to see Gar standing by the burning mast. The sky opened up and rain pelted down.

"We're over here, Gar." Josefina waved her hand in the air, getting his attention.

"Thank God, you are all right." Just that split second of distraction caused Gar not to see a pirate sneaking up behind him, raising his dagger to slit Gar's throat.

"Nay!" cried Josefina, frozen and unable to move. Everything seemed to move in slow motion. Then, to her grateful surprise, Cup swung down on a line, knocking into the pirate, setting him off balance. Gar turned around and slit the pirate's throat.

"Don't look, Etta," said Josefina, cringing and pulling the girl to her.

"Thanks, Cup," said Gar with a nod.

"I do what I can," said the young boy, gripping a dagger but not having had to use it, thanks to Gar.

"Cap'n, there is another ship on the horizon," called out

Solobow, making Josefina's gut wrench. Another pirate ship wasn't what she wanted to hear. This was awful.

"It's flying the flags of the Cinque Ports," shouted T-Bald. The rest of the crew heard him and cheered.

"Thank God," said Gar, running over to Josefina and Etta. "We'll have a chance now," he told them. "But this ship is burning fast and might even sink. Stay behind me, both of you. We'll make our way to the sterncastle and I'll try to get you aboard the Cinque Ports ship as soon as I can." He turned and started walking and fighting off more men at the same time. "Stay close," he commanded.

"We will. Come on, Etta," said Josefina, reaching for the girl's hand.

"Nay. Banshee jumped out of my arms and I have to find her." Etta took off at a run.

"Nay, Etta. Come back here," cried Josefina, trying to stay close to Gar as they headed for the sterncastle of the ship. She wanted to call out and tell Gar the girl was gone, but another distraction was only going to get Gar killed. Josefina didn't know what to do. Hopefully, the Cinque Ports ship would be the answer to their prayers. As soon as the pirates were under control, she'd tell Gar and they'd look for Etta together.

Gar felt new energy, knowing help was on its way. He glanced over to see the Confederation of the Cinque Ports ship getting closer. His uncle— his father was near the bowsprit, getting ready to jump aboard the *Lady Josefina* as soon as he was close enough to do it. Gar felt a wash of relief sweep through him. Mayhap he could get the girls out of this alive after all.

"Gar!" cried Josefina, once again taking his attention.

"What now?" He turned around to find a pirate holding Josefina with a blade to her throat. Her back was toward the man.

"What have we got here?" asked the pirate, smiling and showing his rotten teeth. "A pretty young thing like this aboard a ship?"

"Release her!" commanded Gar. "I won't let you hurt her."

"Not on your life, matey." The pirate laughed. "I'm takin' her back to the ship to enjoy her. Now, out of my way or I'll slit her throat right now, I swear I will."

"Cap'n, help!" It was Cup. He was on the other side of Gar trying to outrun a pirate, but the pirate had him cornered. Cup's back was against the bottom wall of the sterncastle. He held his dagger out with two shaking hands for protection.

"I'm goin' to kill the runt," said the pirate, raising his sword and stepping closer to Cup.

Gar had two people who needed his help now and he cared for them both. He could possibly save one, but not both. He would have to choose Josefina, as much as it pained him not to help the boy since the boy saved his life. God's eyes, how could he save them both?

"There came a blood-curdling screech and something fell from the sterncastle right atop the pirate who was about to kill Cup. It was Banshee. The cat clawed at the pirate's face and the pirate shouted.

"Get this damned thing off of me." He tried to brush the

animal away, but its claws and teeth kept the man from killing Cup. It was just the distraction Gar needed. Cup took advantage of the situation and bravely stabbed his dagger into the man's chest. At the same time Gar shot forward to save Josefina. He knocked the blade out of the pirate's hand and pulled Josefina toward him, at the same time, sinking his sword into the pirate's heart. Just that fast, both of the attackers were dead.

Etta ran down from the sterncastle, collecting her cat. "I threw Banshee at that pirate to save my brother," said Etta, kissing the cat, making sure she wasn't hurt.

"Your brother?" asked Gar.

"Wilmetta? Is that really you?" Cup ran over and the two of them hugged. "Thank you for saving my life."

"It's the Cinque Ports," yelled one of the pirates. "Retreat, retreat!"

By now, the Cinque Ports ship had sailed up, blocking the path of the pirate ship, and boarding the *Lady Josefina*, coming to their rescue.

"Gar! Are you all right?" Gar's father, Garrett Blackmore, ran to him, taking down a pirate along the way. His men quickly boarded the pirate ship as well as the *Lady Josefina*. There was a second Cinque Ports ship approaching as well.

"Aye, Father, we are fine," said Gar, finally lowering his sword. "You are truly a welcome sight."

"This ship is unsafe. We'll have to put out this fire, but in the meantime I want everyone over to the *Champion*," he said, speaking of his ship.

"What about the pirates?" asked Gar.

"I've brought enough men to get that under control.

ELIZABETH ROSE

They'll be put in chains and be brought to trial. Some of my men will sail the pirate's ship back to port."

"The *Lady Josefina* snapped a tiller rope and cannot steer," Gar told him.

"We'll tow her in," said Garrett. "It's a shame since she was such a beautiful ship. It'll take a hell of a lot of work to fix her up."

"I know," said Gar letting out a deep sigh, looking at the ship of his dreams going up in smoke. The odd part was, he wasn't as upset about it as he thought he'd be. All that mattered to him now was that Josefina and Etta were not harmed. He pulled Josefina to him, giving her a kiss atop the head. Then he reached over and ruffled Etta's hair. "I am thankful that none of you were hurt," he told them. Then he looked up at Cup and nodded. Cup smiled and nodded back.

"Cap'n, we're saved," shouted Rusty, running over with Solobow right behind him.

Gar looked up, seeing so many dead bodies and shook his head. This wasn't at all how this trip was supposed to go.

"What's the death count?" asked Gar.

"Cap'n, we've got about a dozen men wounded," announced Solobow.

"What about the dead?" he asked once again.

"Besides who is here, the living consists of T-Bald, Wilkens, and Two-Spit," Rusty informed him.

Gar looked over to see Two-Spit down on the ground, staring at the body of his good friend, Hothead Harry.

"Josefina, you and Etta go with Solobow to the Cinque Ports ship. I'll join you there shortly as soon as we take care of the dead and put out the fire."

242

"I'll watch them good," said Solobow, taking Etta by the hand. Her cat mewed in her arms. "Come on, Josefina."

Josefina's gaze followed Gar's over to Harry. "He saved my life," she said in a mere whisper.

"Mine too," said Gar. "I'll make sure the bodies of the crew are brought back for a proper burial. However, the dead pirates will be buried at the bottom of the sea."

Gar walked over, putting his hand on Two-Spit's shoulder and reaching down to close Harry's eyes.

"Thank you, Baron Blackmore," Josefina told Gar's father.

"Just doing my job as Lord Warden of the Cinque Ports," said Gar's father with a nod. "I'm sorry about your ship," he told her, knowing exactly who she was as well as being acquainted with her father and late husband.

"I'm not," she said, surprising everyone with her answer.

"Josefina, what are you saying?" asked Rusty. "This is your ship and without it you'll have no way to continue the business."

"I don't want to do this anymore," she said, emotion overwhelming her as she watched Gar, thinking how close she'd been to losing him. "I don't want anything to do with pirates or ships or the sea, ever again."

CHAPTER 20

Three days later, Josefina stood next to Gar at the St. Stanislaw cemetery, where many were gathered to pay their last respects to the crew who had died and were buried here. Etta and Cup were inseparable since being reunited, and Banshee was keeping them all busy as they constantly chased after her.

Josefina's brother-by-marriage, Clovis, had come to pay his respects as well. His leg was wrapped up and he used a crutch to walk, while being helped by his wife, Amelia.

"I'm sorry about the ship," Gar told both Clovis and Josefina. "I wish I could have done a better job protecting her."

"It's not your fault, Gar." Josefina gently put her hand on his arm. "Besides, you were protecting us and the crew and that was much more important. I'm just glad we weren't all killed by the pirates."

"Still, I was captain. I feel responsible."

ELIZABETH ROSE

Josefina could tell how upset Gar was by what happened.

"I hear the ship is repairable," said Clovis. "Josefina, you father is going to have one last job before he decides he's too old to build ships anymore."

"I'm sure he'll be happy to do it. He loves building ships as much as Gar loves to sail them."

"Is that so?" asked Clovis.

"I'm not so sure anymore. Excuse me, I see my father and need to talk with him." Gar left, leaving Josefina behind.

"Josefina, as soon as I'm healed, I'll be able to help out more with the business," said Clovis.

"Well, you're going to have to find someone else to do my part because I won't be doing it anymore."

"My dear, what does that mean?" asked Amelia.

"It means, I don't care to run Donald's business anymore."

"What will you do for money?" asked Clovis.

"I have other skills. I'm sure I'll find something that is a lot less dangerous. After all, I have two children now," she said with a smile, nodding to Cup and Etta. "And a cat. Don't forget the cat."

"You're going to raise two children by yourself?" asked Amelia.

"Well, I had hoped not to be by myself, but I think that is not up to me." She turned to see Gar in deep conversation with his father. She probably shouldn't be so curious but she wanted to know what they were talking about. "Pardon me," she said and walked up to join them.

His father looked up when she approached and stopped

talking. Gar turned to look at her but didn't say a word. It was an awkward situation.

"I'm sorry. Am I interrupting something?" asked Josefina.

"It's fine," said Gar. "I wanted to talk to you, Josefina. About my future."

"Oh," she said. "I'm sorry I haven't paid you yet, but with everything that has been going on, it slipped my mind. I promise I'll get you your money today."

"Nay. That's not what I meant."

"I see." She had a feeling she knew what he meant. "You don't need to say anything, Gar. I accept the fact you are about to marry a noblewoman and that I'll never see you again."

"You do?" His expression was a cross between surprised and disappointed.

"It is what the king commanded," said his father. "It's what he needs to do in order to be allowed to sail again."

"I know, Baron Blackmore." Josefina's heart was breaking but she tried to smile. "It is what's important to Gar. He should do it so he can sail again. He deserves to be happy."

Gar stood open-mouthed not believing his ears. Josefina was saying she accepted the fact that he would marry a noblewoman and that they'd never see each other again? How could she say that after what they'd been through together? Surely, he had to have misunderstood her.

"Josefina, you're saying you are willing to accept the fact

I'll marry a noblewoman and we'll never see each other again?" He had to be sure.

" I— I mean... yes," she said, lowering her head and looking at the ground.

"Well, I'm not," he spat.

Her head snapped up and those concerned big eyes stared right through him.

"You're not?" she asked. "What does that mean?"

"It means I just told my father I am willing to give up sailing forever because I don't want to marry a noblewoman."

Her heart raced. "You are? You don't?"

"Josefina," he said, taking her hands in his. "I love you. However, now I'm not sure you feel the same way about me as I do you."

She found herself tongue-tied and couldn't move, speak, or even breathe. Was Gar really willing to give up what he loved most in life for her? And he said he loved her. What exactly did all this mean?

"Josefina? Say something," said Gar, looking worried.

"Gar, I love you too," she said. "But are you sure you are ready to give up sailing? That is what you love most in life."

"Nay. Not true. I love you most, Josefina. I love you and want to marry you. Will you be my wife?"

"M-marry you?" she asked, her gaze shooting over to Gar's father.

Garrett Blackmore shrugged. "It seems my family is all determined to marry from below the salt and I can't stop it."

"But what will the king say?" asked Josefina. "Won't this cause problems?"

"I have a good relationship with the king," said Garrett.

"I'm sure in time I can convince King Edward to let Garrett become a member of the Confederation of the Cinque Ports. After all, he proved he wasn't a pirate by helping to bring in that ship of pirates we've been after for quite some time now."

"Hah!" said Gar. "It's not like I did it on purpose."

"What about the *Lady Josefina*?" asked Josefina. "Won't you want to sail her again someday, Gar?"

"You're the only Lady Josefina I want," said Gar, seeming uneasy. "Josefina, if you don't want to marry me—"

"Yes!" she said excitedly, ready to jump up and down.

"Yes... what?" asked Gar, being cautious.

"Yes, I'll marry you. I do. I want to. I want to marry you more than anything in life."

"You do?" he asked, sounding as if he needed to have it confirmed once more.

Instead of answering, she reached up and kissed him deeply on the mouth, right in front of his father.

"What's this?" asked Gar's mother, Lady Echo, walking up holding Etta's cat. Etta and Cup were with her.

"Mother, Josefina and I are getting married," Gar announced.

Josefina was surprised that his mother didn't even flinch.

"Congratulations," said Echo. "Finally, my eldest son is getting married and I couldn't be happier. I don't know you well, Josefina, but you seem like a woman who will keep my son in line, and I like that."

"Echo," said her husband in a warning voice.

"I mean, you two are perfect for each other," said Echo with a giggle.

"So, you're going to be my new father after all?" asked Etta, tugging at Gar's sleeve.

"Aye. I suppose so," he said, putting his arm around Etta. Josefina noticed Cup looking very sad.

"What about Cup?" asked Josefina.

"What about him?" asked Gar.

"It's all right," said Cup sadly, lowering his head. "I'll continue to live with the surviving crew and working for Clovis."

"Nay, you won't," said Gar.

"I won't?" Cup looked up with a furrowed brow.

"No son of mine is going to live like that. You're coming to the castle with the rest of us."

"That's right," said Garrett. "I told Gar that he and his family are welcome to stay at Saltwood Castle for as long as he wants."

"I'm going to live at a castle?" asked Etta with wide eyes.

"That's right, Etta," Josefina answered.

"What about Banshee?" Worry crossed her face.

"The cat can come too," said Gar. "After all, she's been living with us on the ship and I don't think Etta will go anywhere without her."

"Come, Josefina," said Echo, handing the cat to Etta. "We have much to do to plan your wedding. We want this to be a spectacular event, don't we?"

"Yes, I surely do." She smiled at Gar.

"*We* surely do," he said with a wink. A smile crossed his face that was genuine, and she was sure this is really what he wanted after all.

CHAPTER 21
THREE WEEKS LATER

Josefina clutched her bouquet of wildflowers so tightly that her hands were shaking. Dressed in a velvet royal blue gown with white lace tippets, she wore the clothes of a lady. Today was her wedding day and this time she was marrying the man she loved.

"Josefina, you look beautiful!" Her good friend, Sage, was acting as her maid of honor. Lady Martine, who Josefina had come to know well on their trip, was a bridesmaid. Martine and Sage fixed her long train, as she stood in the courtyard of Saltwood Castle where the wedding was taking place. Normally, it was customary to get married outside of a church. However, since this was Josefina's second marriage and Gar's relatives never seemed to worry about breaking rules, this was where the ceremony would be held.

"Just relax," said Martine seeming so calm. "Everything is going to be fine."

"I'm more nervous now than when I married Donald," Josefina admitted. "Of course, it's probably because this time I'm marrying a nobleman and he happens to be someone I love."

"It's just our brother," said Eleanor, joining them with a tall dark-haired man at her side. "Believe me, there is nothing to be worried about."

"I'm Evan, Gar's brother," said the man with Eleanor.

"So nice to meet you, Lord Evan," said Josefina, trying to curtsey in her gown, almost dropping her bouquet.

"You'd better go," said Martine, waving her hands to make Evan leave. "Only women are supposed to be here."

"I'm going," he said. "I just wanted to meet the bride."

"When are you going to get married, Evan?" asked Martine. "Isn't it past time?"

"Me?" Evan slapped his palm against his chest. "Cousin, you are a year older than me and you're still not married," he told Martine.

"I'll marry someday. When I find the right man." Martine looked the other way and brushed invisible lint off her arm.

"Oh, where is Etta? She is always disappearing." Josefina looked around, feeling frantic. "She is supposed to throw down flower petals as I walk out. And where is my father? He needs to give me away."

"My younger sisters, Regina and Dorothy, are making sure Etta is ready," said Martine.

"And here comes your father now," said Sage, rubbing her pregnant belly.

Josefina waved to her parents, Ernestine and Bartholomew Woods. Her mother was seated and her father, being an older man, made his way over to them slowly. Josefina only had two brothers, so she wouldn't have much family here today.

"Lady Lark wanted to come from Scotland but stayed back because she's pregnant," Martine informed her.

"And our cousins Rook and Raven are unable to make it but send their best wishes," Eleanor relayed the message.

"Oh, how nice." Honestly, Josefina was glad that not all of Gar's aunts, uncles and cousins would be there. She was nervous enough because his mother, a former pirate, and his father, Lord Warden of the Cinque Ports, were there. She kept thinking they were going to stop the wedding from happening, telling her that she wasn't good enough for their son.

"Josie, you are a vision of loveliness." Her father approached her, dressed in his best clothes which were still nothing close to the clothes of a noble. He kissed her on the cheek and took her arm.

"Are Otto and Silas and their families here?" she asked, speaking about her older brothers. "I really want them to be."

"They are. They wouldn't miss attending the wedding of a noble," he said with a chuckle. "Josie, I like Lord Gar. I like him a lot. I believe you're going to be happy this time around. He seems like a good man."

"He is, Father. And yes, I am already extremely happy. I am in love."

"Are you ready to get married? Your groom is waiting."

"Yes, Father," said Josefina, heading across the courtyard holding on to her father's arm. Martine and Sage followed close behind while Etta was guided forward by Martine's sisters to throw flower petals where Josefina walked. The little girl was so cute. She held a basket of petals and in the basket sat her cat, mewing loudly.

Gar looked up as the minstrels started playing music. His eyes fastened on his beautiful bride and his heart swelled. It was truly the right move to give up sailing because he loved Josefina more than any trip on the water or any ship. He wanted to stay on land now, raising a family with his new wife. Every minute away from her was a minute too long.

"Well, you're finally doing it, although we were all starting to wonder if you ever would," whispered Robin, who was his best man.

"We were taking bets on how many grandchildren we would all have before you ever married," said Evan softly. Both of them chuckled at the jest.

"I'm not going to let even you two fools upset me today," said Gar, taking a deep breath and releasing it slowly.

Josefina approached and the music stopped. Then her father kissed her and sat next to his wife.

"You look exquisite, Josefina," Gar told her, unable to keep his eyes off of her. She was dressed in the gown of a lady. He was sure it was his sister's gown, but he didn't even care. Once they were married, Gar would make sure Josefina had plenty of new clothes to wear. After all, she would be his wife and also be granted the courtesy title of Lady.

"I really wanted to sew a gown from the silk I had left from the trade show, but the smoke from the fire on the ship ruined all my cargo," Josefina whispered to him.

"You are beautiful to me in whatever you wear. I

wouldn't even care if you wore nothing at all," he said, getting a slap on the shoulder from Robin and a mean scowl from the priest. "Oh, I didn't mean it that way."

"Can we start?" asked the priest.

"Please do," answered Josefina, most likely speaking up before he said anything else embarrassing.

They exchanged their vows and prayers were recited. Then it was time for the rings.

"Where's Cup with the rings?" asked Gar, afraid giving the boy such an important job was a mistake. Still, he'd wanted to include him in the ceremony since Cup would now be their son.

"I'm here," said Cup, hurrying up to them, holding out a goblet.

"I don't want a drink, I want our rings," Gar grumbled.

"I know. Look inside the goblet."

Gar peeked over the rim to find both rings inside the empty vessel. He smiled, figuring this was Cup's way of adding his personal touch to the ceremony, since he'd been pouring drinks for a crew for most of his life.

He slid the ring onto Josefina's finger and she put his on him. Then they kissed and the crowd clapped and cheered as the minstrels started up a lively tune.

"You are all invited to join us for the wedding ceremony feast in the great hall," called out Gar's father.

The crowd moved slowly toward the great hall, many coming up to congratulate them before they left.

"Son." Garrett approached, holding out his hand. "Con-gratulations." They shook and then Gar's mother gave both Gar and Josefina big hugs.

"Who ever thought anything good could come from a pirate ship?" asked Echo.

"Mother!" Gar frowned.

"I meant, from the pirate attack. On the sea," she explained, looking up at her husband for help.

"What your mother means, is that when the pirates attacked it was probably the time when you realized just how much you loved Josefina," said Garrett.

"Yes, you're right, Mother," said Gar. "I was so afraid of losing her, that I realized she was the most important person in my life."

"Thank you, Husband." Josefina kissed Gar. "You are the most important person in my life as well. I can't wait to start our new life together."

Garrett cleared his throat. "Speaking of new lives, I spoke with King Edward on your behalf."

"You did?" asked Gar feeling the knot back in his stomach. "What did he say? Is he angry with me?"

"Not any worse than with the rest of your cousins and sister for marrying below the salt. As a matter of fact, he was so impressed when he heard how you killed off so many pirates that he wants you to join the Confederation of the Cinque Ports as soon as you are settled and ready."

"He does? Really?" Gar couldn't contain his excitement.

"That means you'll be sailing again, doesn't it?" Josefina asked him.

"Well, yes, it does," he told her. "But not all the time, I swear. And I can defend myself against pirates, so you don't need to worry about me, sweetheart."

"Of course, I'll worry. But since I won't be there to

distract you, I know you will be fine." Josefina smiled as if she knew some kind of secret.

"Why are you smiling like that?" asked Gar.

"I'm smiling because I'm happy. Also because I can't wait to tell you that once the *Lady Josefina* is fixed up, the ship is yours."

"What?" Gar shook his head, not understanding this in the least. "Nay, Josefina. You said you were going to sell it."

"My father loves that ship almost as much as you do," she told him. "He actually wants to work on it. And he also wants to keep it in the family."

"But what about your brother-by-marriage? Won't he need it for his trade?"

"Not anymore," she said. "His leg will take a long time to heal, plus he lost most of his crew when the pirates attacked. His wife heard about all the dangers we had at sea and she convinced him to only do trade along the coast from now on."

"He'll still need a ship for that," Gar reminded her.

"True. And I gave him the funds that we collected from the trade fairs to put toward it. In time, when his leg is healed, he'll find another ship and also another crew. Actually, Solobow, Two-Spit, Whiney Wilkens, T-Bald and Crusty Rusty are all going to help out Clovis on land until they have a ship again. T-Bald even said he hopes to sail with you again someday."

"Aye. I'd like that," said Gar, looking up to first notice all these men were here attending the wedding. They stayed to the back of the crowd. "Isn't that the crew?" he asked stretching his neck, thinking he was mistaken at first. They were all clean and shaven and wore fresh, new clothes.

"That's them," said Garrett. "They said they feel uncomfortable around nobles and looking like that, so they are more or less hiding in the back and getting drunk."

They all laughed at that.

"Gar, are you sure you don't mind if we are Cup and Etta's new parents?" asked Josefina.

"Mind it?" asked Gar. "I love it. Now, I'll have more children than any of my married cousins. After all, I'm the eldest, so I should have the most children, don't you agree, Father?"

"Will you raise them as nobles?" asked Garrett.

"Of course," said Gar. "Now that Josefina is titled, my children will share titles too. Actually, if you don't mind, I'd like to ask Cyprian to do a special job at the castle."

"Who?" asked Garrett.

"He's speaking of the orphan boy," said Echo. "Their new son."

"Yes," said Josefina. "Everyone calls him Cup and his sister, Etta but their real names are Cyprian and Wilmetta."

"I see," said Gar's father. "And what type of job did you have in mind for the boy?"

"Cupbearer, of course," said Gar with a smile. "I mean, he's already more than qualified."

They all laughed heartily at that.

"I agree," said Garrett.

"I think Cup will be happy about it, and it is the perfect position for him," agreed Josefina.

"Mother and Father, did you ever think I'd marry such a beautiful, wonderful, amazing woman?" Gar kissed his new bride.

"We actually never thought you'd marry," mumbled his father, looking off into the distance.

"Honey, that's not true," said Lady Echo. "After all, we always knew how strong Gar was. Just like his father. Both his fathers." She smiled gently.

"I knew as soon as I saw you and Josefina still alive on that ship that you'd end up together," admitted Garrett.

"Why is that?" asked Gar.

"Because, Son," said Garrett, "I found your mother, my true love, on a ship in the midst of pirates, as well. And no matter how tough life gets, a Blackmore is a true survivor and will never have trouble ***Riding out the Storm***."

FROM THE AUTHOR

I hope you enjoyed Josefina and Gar's journey together and will take the time to leave a review for me.

When I first had the idea of nobles marrying commoners in the Below the Salt Series, I had no idea so many of the cousins and siblings from the Blake family would be following in line. Some of my readers have been asking about Lady Martine who is first seen in Winter's Sage. They like her and want her to have her own story. I've decided yes, Martine does need a love of her own. You can find her story in the book that follows this called *Sweet Mead for Lady Martine*. And yes, as you've probably guessed, she is going to fall in love with a commoner who is an innkeeper.

For those of you who are not familiar with my series, the Below the Salt Series is second-generational, meaning it is about the grown up children from my main characters, the Blake family from my Legacy of the Blade Series.

In this book you've heard about Gar's parents, Lord

Garrett Blackmore and his ex-pirate mother, Lady Echo. If you'd like to read their story, you can do so in **Lady of the Mist**, Book 4 of the **Legacy of the Blade Series**.

If you've missed the stories leading up to this, here is a list:
Below the Salt Series:

Picking up the Gauntlet – Book 1 (Lady Raven is the daughter of Corbett and Devon from Lord of the Blade.)

A Rose Among Thorns – Book 2 (Lord Rook is Raven's twin brother.)

Love Letters for Lady Lark – Book 3 (Lark is the daughter of Storm MacKeefe and Wren from Lady Renegade.)

Dancing on Air– Book 4 (Lady Eleanor is the daughter of Garrett Blackmore and Echo from Lady of the Mist.)

Winter Sage– Book 5 (Lord Robin is the son of Madoc (Echo's twin brother) and Abbey from Lord of Illusion.)

Riding out the Storm– Book 6 (Gar is the son of Echo and stepson/nephew of Garrett from Lady of the Mist.)

Sweet Mead for Lady Martine – Book 7 (Lady Martine is the daughter of Madoc and Abbey from Lord of Illusion.)

Watch for possibly more books in the future.

You can follow me on social media, and learn more about the books I write by using the following links:

Stop by and visit my **Website**. You can follow me on **Amazon, Bookbub, Goodreads, Facebook** and **Twitter**. I also have a **Private Readers' Group** on Facebook that I invite you to join.

If you would like to stay informed of my new books and also sales, please be sure to subscribe to my **newsletter**.

Thank you,
Elizabeth Rose

ALSO BY ELIZABETH ROSE

Medieval Series:

Legendary Bastards of the Crown Series

Seasons of Fortitude Series

Secrets of the Heart Series

Legacy of the Blade Series

Daughters of the Dagger Series

MadMan MacKeefe Series

Barons of the Cinque Ports Series

Holiday Knights Series

Highland Chronicles Series

Pirate Lords Series

Highland Outcasts

Medieval/Paranormal Series:

Elemental Magick Series

Greek Myth Fantasy Series

Tangled Tales Series

Portals of Destiny

Contemporary Series:

Tarnished Saints Series

Working Man Series

Western Series:

Cowboys of the Old West Series

And More!

Please visit http://elizabethrosenovels.com

ABOUT ELIZABETH

Elizabeth Rose is an award-winning, bestselling author of over 100 books and counting. She writes medieval, historical, contemporary, paranormal, and western romance. Her books are available as EBooks, paperbacks, and some audiobooks as well.

Her favorite characters in her works include dark, dangerous and tortured heroes, and feisty, independent heroines who know how to wield a sword. She loves writing 14th century medieval novels, and is well-known for her many series.

Elizabeth loves the outdoors. In the summertime, you can find her in her secret garden with her laptop, swinging in her hammock working on her next book. Elizabeth is a born storyteller and passionate about sharing her works with her readers.

Please be sure to visit her website at **Elizabethrosenovels.com** to read excerpts from any of her novels and get sneak peeks at covers of upcoming books. You can follow her on **Twitter, Facebook, Goodreads** or **BookBub.** Be sure to sign up for her **newsletter** so you don't miss out on new releases or upcoming events.

Click to join **Elizabeth Rose's Readers' Group.**